THE SLATER SISTERS OF MONTANA

Nestled in the Rocky Mountains,
the idyllic Lazy S Ranch is about to
welcome home the beautiful Slater sisters.

Don your Stetson and your cowboy boots
and join us as these sisters experience
first loves, second chances and their very own
happy-ever-afters with the most delicious heroes
in the West. No dream is too big in Montana!

Out first in August 2013, don't miss

THE COWBOY SHE COULDN'T FORGET

followed by the second in this fabulous series
in November 2013!

D1134201

Dear Reader

I'm so excited to begin this new series, *The Slater Sisters of Montana*. My stories will be set in the beautiful state of Montana at the Lazy S Ranch.

Patriarch Colton Slater fell in love thirty years ago with Lucia Delgado and they had four lovely daughters: Analeigh, twins Josephina and Vittoria, and Marissa. Then, only a year after the last child was born, Lucia took off—leaving a bitter Colt to raise the young girls alone.

My first story begins when Colt has a stroke and Ana returns home to take care of her father. She quickly learns that the Lazy S is in financial trouble. With ranch foreman Vance Rivers she teams up to work on solutions for the problem together.

Vance was the kid Colt took in as a teenager, and for nearly all that time he has been in love with Ana. Maybe she'll finally notice him?

Ana's concentration is on trying to get her sisters to come home and help out, but they're busy with their own careers. That's understandable, since Colt didn't pay much attention to them as children. She's glad she has Vance to lean on, and quickly discovers what a special man he is.

I hope you enjoy this trip to southern Montana with the Slater sisters.

Patricia Thayer

THE COWBOY
SHE COULDN'T
FORGET

BY
PATRICIA THAYER

Originally born and raised in Muncie, Indiana, **Patricia Thayer** is the second of eight children. She attended Ball State University, and soon afterwards headed West. Over the years she's made frequent visits back to the Midwest, trying to keep up with her growing family.

Patricia has called Orange County, California, home for many years. She not only enjoys the warm climate, but also the company and support of other published authors in the local writers' organisation. For the past eighteen years she has had the unwavering support and encouragement of her critique group. It's a sisterhood like no other.

When she's not working on a story, you might find her travelling the United States and Europe, taking in the scenery and doing story research while thoroughly enjoying herself, accompanied by Steve, her husband for over thirty-five years. Together, they have three grown sons and four grandsons. As she calls them: her own true-life heroes. On rare days off from writing you might catch her at Disneyland, spoiling those grandkids rotten! She also volunteers for the Grandparent Autism Network.

Patricia has written for over twenty years, and has authored more than forty-six books. She has been nominated for both a National Readers' Choice Award and the prestigious RITA® Award. Her book NOTHING SHORT OF A MIRACLE won an *RT Book Reviews* Reviewers' Choice award.

A longtime member of Romance Writers of America, she has served as President and held many other board positions for her local chapter in Orange County. She's a firm believer in giving back.

Check her website, www.patriciathayer.com, for upcoming books.

Recent books by Patricia Thayer:

HER ROCKY MOUNTAIN PROTECTOR
SINGLE DAD'S HOLIDAY WEDDING
THE COWBOY COMES HOME*
ONCE A COWBOY...**
TALL, DARK, TEXAS RANGER**
THE LONESOME RANCHER**
LITTLE COWGIRL NEEDS A MUM**

*The Larkville Legacy
**The Quilt Shop in Kerry Springs

To my good friend and fellow writer Janet Cornelow.
The plotting group will never be the same without you.

CHAPTER ONE

ANA GRIPPED A handful of the horse's mane, lowered her head and gave the animal its lead as she flew over the dew-soaked meadow.

She felt the sting of the cool Montana air against her cheeks, but didn't stop. If she did she was afraid she'd fall apart. And Analeigh Maria Slater was always composed and calm. She had to be. She was the oldest daughter, and since her mother's desertion, the responsibility of her younger sisters had fallen on her shoulders.

Finally reaching her destination, she slowed her horse. The buckskin mare was reluctant to end the run, but obeyed by the time they reached the old, dilapidated cabin. The place Ana had come to as a kid when she needed to be alone, or needed to think. When she needed to cry.

She climbed off, and her legs nearly gave out as she hit the ground. It had been a while since she'd ridden, and she'd pushed it hard today. After tying the mare's reins to the post, she climbed the single step onto the sagging porch. Using her shoulder, she nudged open the weathered door and walked inside.

The cabin was just as dismal as she remembered. The one room was small, but serviceable. A sink and a water pump, a shelf overhead that still held canned goods. There was a set of bunks attached to the opposite wall, with filthy mattresses. The building would have been torn down, but her great-great-grandfather had built it when he'd settled in this area.

She walked to the one window and looked out at the view she loved. The lush meadow was green with new spring grass and wildflowers. She shifted her gaze to the side to see the Rockies, then in the other direction toward Pioneer Mountain and the national forest. In between were miles and miles of Slater land. Colton Slater's pride and joy, the Lazy S Ranch.

And at one time this ranch had been home to Ana and her three sisters. That had been a long time ago.

She brushed a tear from her cheek. But now with her father's emergency… Another tear followed. What was going to happen? What if Colt didn't survive?

She tensed at the sound of another horse approaching, then boots on the porch. She swung around, but didn't feel any relief on seeing the ranch foreman, Vance Rivers, stepping through the doorway.

The man was tall, with wide shoulders. Over the years, she'd caught sight of him without a shirt when he'd been digging fence posts. He'd earned the muscular chest and arms. Her gaze moved down to his flat stomach and narrow waist.

A black Stetson hid most of his sandy hair and shaded those deep-set, coffee-brown eyes that seemed to pierce right through her. She hated that he made her feel nervous and edgy whenever he got near.

"I figured I'd find you here."

"Now that you have, you don't need to hang around," she told him, and turned away. He had been the one who'd called her early this morning about her father's stroke. He also had been the one she found in the hospital room.

Of course that was who her father would want with him. "Shouldn't you be at Colt's bedside?"

Vance had always hated that Ana Slater could make his gut twist into knots. All that thick ebony hair and flawless olive skin showed off her Hispanic heritage, but her brilliant blue eyes let you know she was a Slater. All he knew was the combination made a perfect package.

He drew a calming breath.

Ana had never liked him much. Too bad he couldn't feel the same about her. "It's you who needs to be there when he wakes up."

Vance watched as she straightened, her shoulders rigid.

"Look, Ana, you're the only family here to make the decisions."

He thought about the other Slater sisters, Josie, Tori and Marissa, scattered after college. Not Ana. She might have left the ranch, but only to move into town and take a counseling job at the high school. Close enough so she could come out and check on the old man. On occasion, she saddled a favorite mount and went riding.

Ana finally turned around to face him. He expected to see anger, but instead he saw sadness mixed with fear in her eyes. Again his body reacted. After all these years this woman still had an effect on him.

He thought back to the day Colt Slater had taken him in, twenty years ago. He'd been barely thirteen. The man gave him a place to live. Vance's first home. Slater had only two rules: work hard and keep your hands off his daughters. No matter how difficult, Vance had kept those rules.

"Do you really think Colt Slater is going to listen to me?" Ana asked. "Besides, I'm not even sure if he can hear me."

"That's why you need to be there. Talk with the doctor and find out what you need to do. A stroke doesn't always mean he can't recover." Hell, Vance had no idea what he was talking about.

She shook her head. "You should be there, Vance. Dad will want to see you."

Although Colt was as close to a father as he'd ever had, he couldn't overstep any more than he already had. Whether Colt knew it or not, he needed his daughters.

"No, he needs his family. You have to get your sisters back here and fast. It's way past time."

It was an hour later when Ana and Vance got the horses back to the barn. Then he'd driven her into Dillon to the hospital, where her father had been airlifted just after dawn that morning.

Ana stood in the second-floor waiting area. She'd just left a voice message for her baby sister, Marissa. Tori and Josie at least took her call. The twins told her to keep them informed, but didn't offer to fly in from California. Both had made excuses about their jobs. So that left any decisions about their father's care up to her. She couldn't blame them. How many times had Colt Slater overlooked, rebuffed and just plain ignored these girls?

"Miss Slater?"

Ana turned around and saw the neurologist, Dr. Mason, walking toward her. "Has something changed with my father's condition?" she asked anxiously.

"No, he's remained stable since he was brought in this morning, and the test results are encouraging. I'm not saying that the stroke didn't cause damage to his right side and his speech, but it could have been much worse. He was lucky he got to the hospital so quickly."

Ana was relieved and thankful to Vance, since he'd been with Colt. "Thank you, Doctor. That's great news."

"He's not out of the woods yet. He'll need extensive

rehab to bring him back completely. We would like him to go to a rehab facility to help with improving his motor skills and his speech."

"Good luck with that," Ana said. "No one gets Colt Slater to do anything he doesn't want to do."

"Then you'd better start convincing him he needs this," the doctor suggested.

Before Ana could say any more the elevator doors opened and Vance stepped off.

As much as she hated that he was around, she knew if her father would listen to anyone it would be Vance. Sadness washed over her as she recalled the times Vance had gotten the one-on-one attention she and her sisters had begged for.

He strolled toward them with confidence; add in a little arrogance and you've got Vance Rivers, Ana thought.

"Ana. Doctor." He looked back at her. "Has something happened to Colt?"

"No, in fact it's better than I'd hoped." She went on to explain the doctor's rehab plan. "You need to get him to agree to go."

Vance just stared at her. "What makes you think I have any influence?"

"Well, he sure doesn't listen to me."

The doctor raised a hand. "When the time comes, whoever talks to Mr. Slater had better explain how important rehab is to his recovery." He said goodbye and walked away.

Vance wasn't sure why he was involved in this. He had enough to worry about taking care of the ranch. And he needed Colt's input on so many things. For one, he didn't know how to deal with the daughters.

"Look, Ana. You shouldn't have to handle this on your own. When are your sisters getting here?"

She shook her head. "They aren't coming back for a while."

"What do you mean?"

"Just what I said—they can't get home...right now. They want me to keep them informed."

Vance knew deep down that Colt had never been close with his girls. He more or less let Kathleen handle anything that had to do with the females. The housekeeper and one-time nanny had been with the family for over twenty-five years.

"Then let's go see Colt," Vance said. "For the first time ever, I'm hoping he's his usual cranky self."

Colton Slater blinked and opened his eyes, trying to adjust to the brightness. He glanced around the unfamiliar room. He saw the railing on the bed, heard the monitor. A hospital? What happened? He closed his eyes and thought back to his last memory.

It had been dawn. He'd walked out to the barn to feed the livestock. His arm had been hurt like a son of a bitch since he'd gotten out of bed; then he'd started to feel dizzy and had to sit down on a straw bale. Vance was suddenly beside him, asking him if he was okay.

No, he wasn't okay. Not when he woke up to find that he was in this bed with a needle in his arm, monitors taped to his chest. Worse, he couldn't move. What the hell was going on?

He tried to speak and the only thing that came out was a groan.

"Mr. Slater? Mr. Slater?" He heard a woman's voice. "You're in the hospital, Mr. Slater. I'm your nurse, Elena Garcia. Are you in pain?"

Again he could only groan.

"I'll give you something to help you."

Colt blinked and focused on the raven-haired beauty, and his breath caught. Seeing her heart-shaped face, those almond eyes, he sucked in a breath and opened his mouth to speak. "Luisa…" he whispered, then there was nothing.

Twenty minutes later, Ana walked into her father's hospital room. She held her panic in check on seeing the monitor and the IV connected to the large man in the bed.

She made her way closer. Colt Slater had always been bigger than life to her. The one-time rodeo star was nearly six feet tall, and muscular. The years of ranch work had kept him in shape. His brown hair was now streaked with gray, but even with the tiny lines around his eyes, he was still a handsome man. And she loved him. Maybe in his own way he loved her and her sisters, too. She felt a tear on her cheek and brushed it away.

"Oh, Daddy." She reached out and took his big hand, thrilled that it felt warm. She wanted another chance to get close to this man. Would he be around for that?

A nurse walked in and smiled. "Hello. It's good to see Mr. Slater has a visitor."

"How has he been?" Ana asked.

"He was awake not long ago."

Ana felt hopeful. "Really? Did he say anything? I mean, was he able to speak?"

Again the nurse smiled. "He said the name Luisa. Is that you?"

Ana gasped at hearing her mother's name. "No, it's not." She released her father's hand and hurried out of the room. Oh, God. He still wanted her mother. Ana couldn't stop the tears once she reached the visitors' room and found it empty. She finally broke down and began to sob.

Suddenly she felt a hand on her shoulder, then heard the familiar voice. She wiped her eyes and slowly turned around to see Vance. His dark gaze locked on hers and she saw the compassion. He didn't speak as he slowly drew her close. God help her, she went into his arms, letting his strength absorb the years of pain and hurt. She gripped his shirt and buried her face against his chest and sobbed.

Vance fought not to react to this woman. That was like saying not to take his next breath. Not to ache for something he'd wanted for so long and knew he couldn't have. Now, sweet Analeigh was in his arms.

The top of her head barely reached his chin, and it seemed every curve was pressed against him, tormenting him. He moved his hands over her back, feeling her delicate frame. She might feel fragile but she was far from it. He'd watched for years how she'd corralled her siblings, broke up fights, helped with school projects and even stood up to Colt for them.

He'd never seen her so broken as right now. "Hey, bright eyes, what's wrong? Is Colt worse?"

Vance reached in his back pocket, pulled out his handkerchief and handed it to her. She took it, but kept her head down. "C'mon, tell me," he coaxed. "Is it Colt?"

She shook her head.

"What's breaking your heart, Ana?"

She finally looked up at him. Her eyes welled with tears, her face was blotchy, but she looked beautiful. "He said her name."

Vance frowned. "Whose name?"

"My mother's. He said Luisa."

Vance wasn't shocked. "He's had a stroke, Ana. The man might be confused with the place and time."

She nodded, and as if she realized their closeness, she took a step back. "You're probably right. Sorry. It's just he hasn't said anything about our mother in years. I thought he'd gotten over her." She pointed to Vance's wet shirt. "I'll wash it for you."

Vance wondered if it was possible to wash her out of his head, his heart.

It had been a long day by the time Vance brought Ana back to the ranch. He drove up the circular drive and let her out of the truck. Then he took off toward the barn to check on the stock and the ranch hands.

Ana stood there and looked up at the large ranch house. It had been months since she'd been inside, but when the housekeeper, Kathleen, insisted she stay over tonight, she didn't have a choice.

She walked up the steps to the wraparound porch. Colt had built this house for his new bride, Luisa Delgado. It was well known about her parents' whirlwind romance, also about Luisa's disappearance twenty-four years ago.

Ana had been five years old at the time. She made herself remember the loving woman who'd hugged and kissed her little girls endless times. The woman who told those made-up bedtime stories, sat with her daughters when they were sick.

Not the woman who'd one day up and abandoned her family. All of them had been scared, including Colt. So much so, he couldn't even stand to be their father anymore. And today, Ana had realized he still wanted his ex-wife.

She walked through the front door. Everything was the same, including the large table in the entry, adorned with fresh cut flowers from Kathleen's garden. Ana glanced up at the open staircase with the decorative wooden banister, winding up to the second floor. She walked farther into the house, passing the living room. Two overstuffed leather sofas faced the river-rock fireplace. This was definitely a man's room. Her dad's office was next, then came the huge dining room with its high-back chairs and a table that could seat twenty. She moved on to her favorite room, the kitchen.

She smiled and glanced around to see the rows of white cabinets, which had been painted many times over the years to keep their high sheen. The countertops were also white, and the same with the appliances. The room was clean and generic. Long gone were any Spanish influences.

Kathleen walked in from the laundry room. The house-keeper was fifty-five and had a ready smile and kind hazel eyes. Her hair had been dark brown, but over the years had turned gray. She had never married, so Ana and her sisters were like the children she'd never had.

"Oh, Ana, I'm glad you're here. I'm hoping you'll be staying long enough for me to fatten you up. Child, you're too thin."

"I weigh the same as I always did, no more, no less."

Ana wasn't sure staying at the house was a good idea. There were so many memories she wanted to forget. But she'd be closer to the hospital. And since school was out for the summer, she was off work.

"Well, you still need to put on ten pounds."

Before Ana could protest, there was a knock on the back door. Kathleen went and answered it. "Oh, hello, Mr. Dickson."

Ana watched as the older man stepped into the kitchen. The distinguished-looking Wade Dickson was dressed in his usual business suit. He was not only Colt's lawyer, but his longtime friend. They'd gone to school together. And Uncle Wade had given the Slater girls more affection than their own father had.

He smiled when he saw her. "Hello, Ana."

She was still raw from today, and exhausted. "Hi, Uncle Wade."

He came closer and hugged her. "I'm sorry about your daddy. I was out of town when I got the news. But don't worry, old Colt is made of strong stuff."

She was touched. "I appreciate you saying that."

He released a long breath and guided her into the dining room, where they sat down at the table.

"I hate to do this, Ana girl, but we need to discuss what to do while your daddy is recovering."

She hated that term. "Vance is foreman. Can't he handle the ranch?"

There was another long pause. She could tell Wade was holding something back. "That's a temporary fix. I've been by the hospital, and right now your father isn't in any shape to make decisions. You girls will have to decide what to do for now."

"Dad will be okay," Ana insisted. "The doctor said… Well, he's going to need some rehab."

"I know, and I hope that will happen, too, but as his lawyer, I have to carry out his wishes. To protect his property and his family. And as of right now, Colton Slater is incompetent to run his business."

Ana felt her heart skip a beat. "So what do I need to do? Sign some payroll checks?"

"Well, first of all," Wade began, "Colt has a will, so he didn't put this all on your shoulders. You have a co-executor to help."

"Who?"

She heard someone talking with Kathleen, then a few heartbeats later, Vance walked into the room. He nodded to Wade. "Have you told her?"

The lawyer turned back to her. He didn't have to speak;

she already knew that her father had picked Vance over his own flesh and blood.

"So you've finally got what you wanted," she said. "Now all you have to do is change your name to Slater."

CHAPTER TWO

VANCE WORKED HARD not to react. He'd had plenty of practice over the years masking his feelings, especially around
Ana.

"I'll let that pass, since I know you're upset. Colt named
me because I've been foreman of the ranch for the past
five years. This has nothing to do with me taking over."

Wade Dickson jumped in. "He's right, Ana. It wouldn't
be any different if your father had appointed me to oversee
things. And believe me, I'm grateful he didn't. Running a
large operation like the Lazy S is a big undertaking, and I
don't think you want to handle that. Do you?"

She didn't back down. "I've never gotten the chance to."
Her angry gaze danced back and forth between the two
men. "Dad didn't have any problem putting his daughters to work. Of course, he made sure we were limited
to mucking out stalls or currying horses. And if we were
really good at our jobs, we got to help with some of the
roundups and branding. Yet once he thought we became a
nuisance, he sent us off to the house."

Vance glanced away. He'd seen over the years how Colt
ignored his daughters. The man had never been demonstra-
tive, but he'd given Vance a chance at a life. Hell, the girls
had been lucky. When their father noticed his daughters
were getting tired, he'd made them stop.

Colt had never been that generous with him. The man was never abusive, but had sometimes worked Vance twelve- to fourteen-hour days when it came to roundup time.

"Colt didn't want you to get hurt," Dickson stated. "Ranching isn't an easy life."

Ana shook her head. "We both know the truth. Colton Slater just wanted sons. And he sure didn't want his daughters involved with his precious ranch." She shot a hard look at Vance. "What about you? Do you have a problem working with a woman?"

He frowned. "What exactly do you mean by *working?*"

She moved around the table. "I've waited twenty-plus years to be able to feel a part of this place. I have the chance and the time, since I'm not going back to work at the school until the fall, and I plan to use it. You can either help me or get out of my way."

Vance wasn't sure he liked Ana's idea. "What are you talking about?"

"You aren't going to have all the say-so around here. Dad gave me at least half control of this place."

Why was she acting as if this was war? "Up till now, the only person who had any control was Colt," Vance argued, trying to keep the anger out of his voice. "He's the boss. I still plan to carry out his wishes, because his situation is temporary. But if you want to work fourteen-hour days and smell like sweat and manure, feel free." He started for the door, but stopped. "Just don't plan for me to babysit you or your sisters, because the Lazy S is depending on this roundup." He turned and walked out.

Ana realized she might have overreacted a little. But Vance Rivers had always been the thorn in her side. There was no doubt that Colt had favored him over his own daughters. Well, not anymore.

She stood a little straighter. "It seems I'm going to be working this summer."

Wade Dickson shook his head. "I think you'd better get on that cowboy's good side, or it's going to make life difficult for the both of you."

That was the last thing she wanted. She hadn't forgotten the teenage Vance, with his bad attitude and swagger. He was good-looking and knew it. That day in the barn when he'd got her alone in the stall and kissed her until she couldn't remember her own name wasn't going to happen again. Nor was she going to run away like a scared rabbit.

Ana blinked, bringing her back to the present. "Dad's stroke is more than making things difficult. But I don't plan on ignoring my responsibilities to him or the ranch."

Wade shook his head. "I hope Colt appreciates your loyalty, but don't be too stubborn to think you can do this on your own. So you might want to find a way to get along with Vance. That's the only way this is going to work." The older man sighed. "Also, it might be a good idea to stop by my office tomorrow. There are some more details to go over."

"What details?" she asked.

"It can wait until tomorrow, but not much longer. Bring Vance with you."

Ana didn't like the sound of that.

"What about your sisters?" Wade asked. "When are they coming home?"

Ana had no idea. "Not right away. So this is on me for now." She tried to sound confident, but in reality she didn't know even where to start.

An hour later in the barn, Vance worked the brush along the flank of his chestnut stallion, Rusty. He was angry, more at himself than with anyone else. He'd let her get to him…again. How many times had he told himself to forget about Ana? The woman wanted nothing to do with him. He couldn't say he blamed her, not when their dad had ignored his girls all those years, while giving Vance the attention they should have gotten.

Many times he'd wanted to let Colt know how he felt about that, but the man had taken Vance in when he had nowhere else to go but into foster care.

Vance already had the stigma of having a father who'd been labeled no good for years. Calvin Rivers was well known as a man who couldn't hold down a job, and drank away his paycheck when he found someone willing to hire him. Vance's mother had gotten fed up and took off.

The strokes of his brush got more intense and Rusty expressed his irritation by dancing sideways in the stall. "Sorry, fella." Vance smoothed a hand over his withers and put the brush away. "I didn't mean to take out it out on you."

He walked out of the stall and headed down the center aisle of the large barn, passing the dozen horses stabled here. He stopped and talked to two of the ranch hands, Jake and Hank, giving them instructions for tomorrow's workday.

He said good-night and went through the wide door into the cool May evening. This had always been his favorite time of day. Work was done. The sun had gone down and the animals were all settled in for the night.

He knew his days on the Lazy S could be numbered. It was past time he left here, especially now that he had his own section of land. He'd already planned to leave in the fall after the alfalfa harvest. Now with Colt's stroke…

He headed along the path toward his place. A hundred yards away was the foreman's cottage. About four years ago, Colt had given him the three-bedroom house when he made Vance ranch foreman, after Chet Anders retired. Vance had been twenty-six and had just finished his college courses for his degree. That had been important to Colt. He was grateful, too.

Vance slowed his pace as he reached the house, seeing a shadow on the porch. He paused, then realized it was Ana sitting on the glider swing. Funny, for years he'd dreamed of her coming to visit him. He doubted this time was for the same reason he'd had in mind.

"You want another strip of my hide?" he asked, then kept walking into the house and flipped on the wall switch to light the compact living room.

He was surprised to see that Ana had jumped up and followed him, but stopped at the threshold. "No, I just want to talk to you about something. If you'll give me a few minutes."

Vance turned around to see the worried look on her face. He'd caught a glimpse of her vulnerability at the hospital today, but she also could have a cutting tongue. But he couldn't seem to take heed to the warning his brain sent as he glanced over her slender body, her rounded hips and long legs incased in worn jeans. He bit back a groan. She had just enough curves to twist a man's gut, making him want what he had no business wanting. Somehow Vance had to stop it if he planned to work with her.

Why couldn't he have these feelings for any other woman but her? Why hadn't he been able to move on? Forget the girl who hadn't cared about him years ago. By the looks of it, her feelings hadn't changed. Ana Slater didn't want him.

He was frustrated as he said, "Whatever I do or say, you attack my character. Even I have limits."

Ana knew her anger had gone too far. It wasn't Vance who caused the problem between her and her father. "I apologize. I let old feelings get in the way of what we need to do. And that's run this ranch."

When he stepped aside, she released a breath and made her way past the overstuffed sofa to look out the window that faced the barn and corral. It was easier than looking at Vance. He made her feel things whenever she got near him. It was strange because it had been years since the man had come close to her. Of course, she hadn't given him a chance.

"So you want to call a truce?" he asked.

She looked over her shoulder and nodded. "Wade pointed out we need to work together." She rushed on. "For the good of the ranch, and to help ease Colt's mind so he can concentrate on his recovery."

"We can't expect miracles."

Ana couldn't help but smile. "I'll settle for getting him to do what he needs to do to get back here." She released a long sigh. "I know you think that I don't care about my father, but I do."

"I never said that. In fact, I know how many times you've come out here and checked on him." Vance raised a hand when she started to deny it. "And no, Kathleen didn't rat you out. I've seen your car up at the house, and when you come by to go horseback riding. Why didn't you ever stay and talk with Colt?"

Tears formed behind her eyes. "That's a little difficult when Dad hasn't exactly welcomed me with open arms."

"Okay, his disposition has always been a little gruff, but maybe you can change that now."

Ana thought back to when life here on the Lazy S, with her mom and dad and younger sisters, had seemed about perfect. That had all changed overnight when Luisa Slater just walked out of their lives. It had been as if all the love was sucked away. The twins, Tori and Josie, were only three years old then. Marissa was barely a toddler.

If they hadn't found the note, they might have believed Luisa had been kidnapped. But no, there was no doubt that the woman wanted out of her marriage and to have no part of her children. That same day, Colt had changed, too. He'd closed up and shut his family out.

"He had four daughters who begged for his love. It's as if he blamed us for our mother's disappearance." Ana glared at Vance. "Were we responsible?"

He shook his head. "I can't answer that, Ana. I never met your mother. I've only dealt with mine. And April Rivers had no trouble packing up and leaving, too."

Ana gasped, realizing how closely their lives paralleled. "I'm sorry, Vance. I forgot."

"That's what I want people to do. Forget about my past." His dark gaze met hers. "It's the only way to move on."

Vance didn't want to rehash his past, because Ana and her sisters had the life of fairy princesses compared to his childhood. "Look, running the Lazy S isn't an easy job." He was aware of the toll it had been taking on Colt the past year. "We have the roundup soon. If you and your sisters want to help out, I'm not going to stop you."

"Like I said, I doubt my sisters will come home, but I plan to be around. In fact, I decided to move back to the house, at least over the summer or until Dad gets better."

Lord help him, Vance wanted Ana to stay around. The downside was she'd be here every day, reminding him of what he could never have.

"Okay, the day starts at 5:00 a.m."

She looked surprised. "I want to go see Dad by ten o'clock. And Wade Dickson wants us to meet him tomorrow afternoon in his office."

"Why?"

"I'm not sure. He said there are things we need to go over."

Vance nodded. "Then I guess you'd better get some sleep. Tomorrow is going to be a busy day."

She nodded. "I'll see you in the morning." She headed to the door.

Vance fisted his hands, wanting to call her back. And for what? To tell her he'd always care about her. That he'd wished those visits to the ranch had been to see him. No. To her, he was only the poor kid Colt had given a place to sleep. Even now, with his success, would she see him any differently?

Maybe over the summer she'd notice he was more than just another ranch hand.

The next morning, Colt felt the warmth of the sunlight on his face. Damn. Had he overslept? He blinked, opened his eyes and tried to focus. That wasn't the worst of his problems. He couldn't move. He groaned as he tried to lift his arm, and felt the touch of a hand, then a voice as someone said his name.

He turned his gaze and stared into her pretty face. He nearly gasped. Then he blinked and realized it was Analeigh. Oh, God, she looked so much like…her mother. No. He didn't want to think about Luisa now. But he knew that wishing wouldn't make it so. He'd given up on ever completely forgetting his wife. Correction, ex-wife.

Colt tried to pull away, but he didn't have the strength. What the hell was happening to him? He tried to speak, but all he managed was another groan.

"It's okay, Dad. We're here with you. You need to be still."

He groaned again.

"Please, Dad. You're in the hospital. You had a stroke, but you're going to be all right."

Colt could only look at her, then he relaxed when someone appeared next to her. Vance.

"Hey, Colt. Glad to see you're awake. The doctors have a handle on this. You'll be home before you know it. Trust me, everything will be all right at the ranch. I'll make sure of it. You just rest for now and get your strength back."

Strength. He was weak as a kitten. He closed his eyes as all the fight left him.

Just before noon, Ana sat in Vance's truck as they headed back to town to see the lawyer. She still couldn't get the picture of her father lying in the hospital bed out of her mind. Her chest was tight with emotion. This had to be hard for a man like Colt. He had always been physical, hardworking. Now, that had all changed. Would he be stuck in a wheelchair the rest of his life?

She thought about when she'd sat by the bed, praying he would open his eyes. Even his angry scowl was better than that blank look. No. She had to think positively. Her dad survived the stroke and he was going to recover.

He still hadn't spoken to anyone, except to say Luisa's name. At least he'd said something.

Ana felt Vance's presence, turned sideways and saw him sipping the coffee he'd gotten from the hospital.

He nodded to the one he'd brought for her. "Have some coffee. You look like you need it."

"Thanks." She reached for the cup in the console and took a sip. "This is good."

He smiled as he concentrated on the road. "Got it from the nurses' station. It's their own private brew."

She could just see Vance Rivers flirting with the nurses to get what he wanted. "Thank you."

"Let's talk," he stated, then went on to say, "It's only been forty-eight hours since Colt's stroke and he's still heavily medicated. You need to trust that he's going to get better."

She glanced out the windshield, watching the open ranch land, mountains for a backdrop. "He looks so helpless."

"Give it time, Ana. You need to be patient and not get your dad riled up."

"Riled up?" That hurt. "I don't plan to upset my father. How can you say that?"

Vance raised a hand from the steering wheel. "I only meant that you're too easy to read. Your emotions show on your face."

"I can't help that."

Vance nodded, knowing Ana had always had trouble hiding her feelings. She had a big heart and that was why it was breaking right now. She wanted so much to help. She'd tried so hard to keep the family together, but in the end her sisters all left anyway.

"You have to try, because Colt needs our help with his recovery."

Vance slowed the truck as they approached the small town of Royerton. Population was about five thousand in the ranching and farming community. He drove along Main Street, passing the small grocery, Quick Mart and the U.S. Post Office.

"And I plan to do exactly that."

"Good. Maybe we should keep the topic on the ranch. But not include that you'll be working with the other ranch hands."

"Like he'd care."

Vance pulled into a parking space outside the brick, two-story professional building. "Are you kidding?" He threw the gearshift into Park. "There were two rules that Colt enforced. One, work hard, and the other, stay away from his daughters."

Seeing Ana's surprised look, Vance retrieved his keys and got out of the vehicle. He wasn't about to tell her how difficult it had been to keep that promise, but he had because of the respect he felt for her dad. He'd been crazy about this woman for years. Could there be a second chance for him?

"I didn't know," she said when he opened the passenger-side door.

"There's a lot about Colt you don't know."

She took Vance's offered hand and stepped down onto the sidewalk. "That's not my fault."

"I didn't say it was." He opened the door to the lawyer's office and let her walk inside first. "I just wanted you to be aware of it."

"What about you? Did that rule apply to you?"

He nodded, wondering if she remembered that one time in the barn.

"Since you're still around, I guess you never told him that you accosted one of his daughters in the barn." She turned her back on him and walked into the reception area.

"Whoa. I wasn't alone that day, or the only one responsible for what happened. If I remember right, there was a certain young girl who'd been sniffing around a young teenage boy. Not a good idea. You know, raging hormones and all."

"I didn't have raging hormones," she retorted.

"Not yours. Mine." He studied the blush on her cheeks. He, too, was remembering the day she'd let him lead her into a stall and kiss her. If one of the other ranch hands hadn't come back early, he wondered how far he could have gone. He started to speak when Wade Dickson came out of his office and greeted them.

"Hello, Ana and Vance." He smiled. "Please come inside."

They went ahead of the lawyer into the adjoining room. Nothing too fancy, but there were nice comfortable chairs and a large desk. Wade had his law degree from the University of Montana hanging on the wall.

"Have a seat." He walked around the desk and sat across from them. He opened a folder and glanced over the contents, then looked at Ana. "Are you sure your sisters can't come home?"

"Not right away. Why?"

"I didn't tell you everything last night. There's a slight problem with the ranch."

Ana slid to the edge of her chair. "What is it?"

"As you know, the Lazy S is a sizable spread." He quoted the section amount. "Your father owns that land outright. But there's a lot of grazing acreage that is leased from the state. And the payment is past due."

"How is that possible?"

"Only Colt knows the answer to that." Wade paused. "I managed to get an extension from the state, but it's only bought us a few months to come up with the money. And if you don't pay it, someone else gets a chance to bid on the property."

Ana glanced at Vance. "Then we need to pay it."

Wade looked worried. "There aren't enough funds available."

CHAPTER THREE

ANA'S EYES WIDENED. "What do you mean, there aren't enough funds?"

Wade leaned back in his chair. "It means the Lazy S has had a rough few years. I just recently learned this because I've been notified by the State Land Leasing Board."

Ana turned to Vance. "Why didn't you say something?"

He was as shocked as she was. "First of all, I didn't know anything about the lease coming due. I knew beef prices were down and that we lost several head in that big storm last winter, but..." He'd never dreamed it had been this bad.

"What do you mean, you didn't know? You're Dad's foreman."

"I may physically run the operation, but Colt funds the business account. I use that money for payroll and for the feed and supplies. Colt kept the ranch finances."

He thought about the land that Colt had given to him a few years back. He'd planted an alfalfa crop on the acreage. It should be ready to harvest in about six weeks. That gave them the time, but would the profit be enough?

Wade broke into his thoughts. "Ana, I've been trying for years to get your father to diversify. He lost a lot of his savings when the market tanked a few years ago. In the past, that money had always been his cushion through the bad years."

Ana looked pale. "What do we do now?"

Vance wished he could offer a miracle, but he wasn't sure there was one. "Like Mr. Dickson said, we have nearly six months." His gaze met hers. "You can't do this on your own. I think you need to get your sisters together."

Thirty minutes later, Vance escorted Ana out of the Dickson law office.

"You look ready to drop," he told her.

"Gee, thanks. What every woman wants to hear."

He ignored her comment. "When was the last time you ate?"

"I had some toast this morning. I'm just not hungry."

"It's after one o'clock. You have a lot to deal with, so you need to eat." He placed his hand on the small of her back and immediately felt the warmth of her skin, but resisted the urge to draw her any closer.

She sighed. "You're right, but I should go home and figure out what to do about this mess."

Nixing her request, he guided her a short distance down the sidewalk to a small family-owned restaurant, the Big Sky Grill.

"First, you're going to eat." He held open the door. When she didn't move, he said, "I can keep this up all day."

She glared at him with those big blue eyes, then finally relented. "Okay. A *quick* lunch."

Once inside, they were greeted by the owners, Burt and Cindy Logan. Burt escorted them across the tile floor to a booth next to the picture window that looked out onto Main Street. Several patrons stopped Ana en route and wished her father well. When she finally got away, she slid into one of the bench seats while Vance sat down across from her and placed his hat on the space beside him. He pulled out a menu from between the salt-and-pepper shakers and went over the choices.

Cindy showed up with two glasses of water. "How's your daddy doin'?" she asked.

"A lot better. He's stable for now, but they're still running more tests."

The middle-aged woman placed her hand on Ana's. "Tell Colt that we're all praying for him."

"He'll appreciate that, Cindy. Thank you."

They gave her their order and she left them alone.

Ana shook her head. "I can't believe how many people care. Funny, isn't it? He seems to have gotten along with everyone except his own daughters."

Vance shrugged. "Why does that surprise you? The Slater family helped settle Royerton. Colt is well respected around here."

Vance knew how Colt had treated his girls. It wasn't that he was mean, he just pretty much ignored them. Over the years, Kathleen had always been the surrogate parent. "Okay, the man wasn't the perfect father." Vance leaned back in the seat. "So why did you stay, and not take off like your sisters?"

Ana stared at him with eyes that were the mirror image of Colt's. "I stayed for my sisters, then I got the job at the high school." She shrugged. "I'm not even sure it matters anymore."

Vance leaned forward. "Look, Ana, I don't know why Colt did a lot of things. There's no doubt he isn't a happy man. I've heard stories about how he was when he was younger, before your mother left."

He watched Ana stiffen.

He wasn't going to be put off. "Do you remember her?"

With a nod, she glanced away. "I was pretty young. But,

yes, I can remember how beautiful she was. Her voice, her touch." She turned back and he saw the tears in her eyes. "I wanted to hate her, but for years I just kept praying she'd come back and be our mom again."

He reached across the table and touched her hand. "That's understandable."

She looked down at his hand and slowly pulled hers away. "Is it? Do you wish your mother would come back?"

"Sure. Every kid does, especially when your dad isn't around to feed you and you're hungry." Vance blew out a breath. "And you can't go to school because you don't have shoes. Kids make fun of you for things like that. But sometimes you're just too hungry to care, when you know you'll get that free meal at lunch."

He caught the look on her face and realized how much he'd disclosed.

This time Ana took his hand. "Oh, Vance. I had...had no idea."

He shrugged it off. "No one did. At fourteen, I finally had enough and was trying to get away. I was big for my age and hoped I could go somewhere and get a job.

"I hid out in the back of a pickup truck in the parking lot so I could get out of town. I didn't know it belonged to Colt until I found myself at the Lazy S. I decided to sleep in the barn before starting my journey in the morning. Of course he found me."

Ana didn't want to feel sympathy for the kid who had a rotten life. "And you became the son Dad always wanted."

"As I told you before, I only wanted to survive," Vance stressed. "Colt was my only way out of a bad childhood. I'm sorry if you thought you had to compete against me for your father's attention."

She shrugged. It all seemed so juvenile now. "It doesn't

matter anymore. Colt made his choices a long time ago and that's why I can't get my sisters to come back here."

"Maybe if they know about the state of the ranch... I mean, it's part of their heritage, too. Their inheritance. Wouldn't they want to preserve it?"

Ana shrugged. "So far they haven't seemed too interested in anything to do with Colt or the ranch." She raised her gaze to meet his. "The trick is, how do I convince Josie, Tori and Marissa to come home?"

"Tell them the truth. Colt needs them and you can't do it all. At the least, you need help with his care." He paused, then asked, "Aren't they all living in California? You could go see them."

"Go there?"

He nodded. "If you show up on their doorstep they have to listen to you. They should help you with medical decisions about your father."

She frowned. "You don't know my sisters." This could backfire in her face. "So I think you should go with me."

The nurse raised Colt's bed so he could finally sit up. What he really wanted was to get the hell out of this place. Not an easy task, since he was still weak as a newborn calf and he couldn't move his right arm.

"Is that better, Mr. Slater?" the nurse, whose name was Erin, asked.

He grunted.

She smiled again as she put the call button next to his good hand. "Press this if you need me. Your daughter will be here, too. Plus, they should be coming to talk to you about your therapy soon."

He grunted again. What good was that going to do?

"It's going to take some work to get back in shape, Mr.

Slater, but you've got a good chance for a full recovery. But you'll need to work hard."

As if he hadn't worked hard all his life.

The nurse turned on the television to a game show, then walked out of the room, leaving him alone.

Most of the time he liked being alone. What choice did he have? Ranch work had filled in a lot of lonely hours. He released a breath and closed his eyes. What was he going to do when he didn't have the Lazy S anymore? Sit in a nursing home somewhere until he died?

Sadness overtook him as he closed his eyes and thought back over his life. His chest tightened when he thought of Luisa.

He could still picture her as vividly as if it were yesterday. Small and delicate, Luisa Delgado was beautiful with all that thick, black hair and large eyes. Her olive skin was flawless. When he first saw her, at a rodeo, he'd thought she was an angel. When she walked up and talked to him, he figured he'd died and gone to heaven.

After they'd married, weeks later, he'd thanked God every day, and especially when they were blessed with the babies, every one of them a beauty like their mother.

The tightness in Colt's chest worsened as he recalled the evening he'd come in from the range, so anxious to see his girls. Luisa had been moody and distant of late, with caring for the children. He'd offered to get her someone to help, but she said she wanted to be their mother full-time. Later that night he'd found her crying, and had asked her what was wrong.

She'd only said, "Just make love to me so all the bad things will go away."

Colt released another sigh, recalling how intense their loving had been that night. When he'd walked into the house the next afternoon, there was a babysitter and his wife was gone. All that he had was a short note, telling him she no longer wanted a life with him and their daughters.

He'd searched for her, wanting to beg her to come home, but he never found her. Then he got the divorce papers. That day his life as he knew it had ended.

Two days later, Vance sat next to Ana as the plane landed at LAX. He had no idea how he'd gotten roped into going to California.

For one thing, he hated large cities and the crowds. Secondly, if there had been any animosity between him and Ana, it had been worse with the younger sisters. He had to just keep remembering he was doing this for Colt, and for Ana.

The plane taxied to the terminal. "I'm not sure this visit will change anything," Ana said, feeling a little nervous. Maybe it had something to do with the close quarters. Vance was a big man, and that didn't leave her much room. "What if Tori and Josie refuse to help?"

"Then we go back to Montana and figure it out on our own." His hand rested against his jean-covered thigh. She was suddenly intrigued by his long, tapered fingers.

He went on to say, "And we will figure out something. I promise."

She glanced at his face and saw his sexy smile. Her heart went *zing* and she had to look away. No! She wasn't going to even think about this man like that. Okay, so maybe it was normal, since she hadn't been in a romantic relationship in a while. That was still no excuse to think about Vance Rivers that way. She was no longer that dreamy-eyed teenage girl who wanted his attention. No way was she getting involved with him.

When the plane stopped at the gate, she unfastened her seat belt as Vance stood and reached up into the overhead compartment. He took down her carry-on and his duffel, along with his cowboy hat. He stepped back to let her out into the aisle. The small space made it impossible not to brush up against him. She inhaled his scent and could feel his hard body. Again the zings. Okay, so that hadn't changed over the years; he still appealed to her, a lot.

Since they had their only luggage with them, they went straight to the car rental booth. Vance got a midsize sedan and started to climb into the driver's seat.

Ana looked at him. "Can you drive the L.A. freeways?"

He took off his hat and tossed it in back. "We'll soon find out."

"Here's the address for Josie's business."

Vance took the paper and entered the address in the GPS, then headed for the 5 Freeway. They ended up in the older section of Los Angeles not far from Griffith Park. It was a two-story stucco building with a Spanish design.

They got out of the car and walked up to the directory on the wall. It didn't take long to find the right office. The sign on the glass door read Slater Style.

"Catchy name," Vance said.

"That's what Josie's all about." Ana released a breath. "Okay, let's get this over with."

Vance nodded, opened the door and allowed her to step in ahead of him. The small reception area consisted of a desk and chairs that lined the opposite walls. But there wasn't a soul in sight.

Vance checked his watch. "I guess everyone's at lunch. Did you tell Josie you were coming?"

"No. I didn't want her to find an excuse to keep me away."

Suddenly the door opened and a familiar woman, carrying a take-out food sack, walked in. However, it wasn't the twin they expected to see here.

Vittoria Slater had dark hair, the same pretty smile as her older sister. "Ana? What are you doing here?"

"Tori?" Ana rushed to her and they hugged tightly. "I think you know my reason for coming to L.A. But what are you doing at Josie's office?"

"Well, as of a few months ago, it's my office, too. I quit my job and decided it was time I went out on my own." She nodded. "Josie offered me office space here. I decided to give my own web-design company a chance."

Tori had their mother's coloring, the olive skin, midnight-dark eyes and ebony hair. Her hair was shorter now, cut just below her chin.

Ana was excited for her sister, knowing how unhappy she'd been with her previous company. But Ana was a little sad that she hadn't shared this with her.

"That's great. So how is business?"

"Good. Several of my old clients came with me, and I like being my own boss." Tori finally noticed Vance across the room and she blinked in surprise. "Vance, good to see you." Her smile faded. "Wait a minute, has something more happened to Colt?"

"No, your dad is still the same," Vance told her. "I'll let your sister explain the rest."

"We need to talk about what to do," Ana stated. "Dad isn't going to get better right away, so we've got to discuss…some things. The ranch, mainly."

The anger was evident in Tori's eyes. "It can dry up and blow away for all I care. I hate that place."

Ana wasn't surprised by her sister's reaction. "Tori, you can't mean that. It's our home."

The younger twin shook her head. "It was just a big, old house to me. Dad was happier when we finally all left."

Ana wasn't surprised by the animosity toward their father. "I understand your feelings, but right now, Colt can't

speak, or make decisions for the Lazy S. I'm going to re-
mind you that the ranch has been in our family for three
generations."

Tori began to speak when the office door opened and
another sister walked in.

"Hey, Tori, it's about time—" Josefina Slater stopped
and stared. "Ana! What are you doing here?"

"Is there an echo in here?" Ana hugged the other twin.
Josie had fair skin with long, golden-brown hair and the
Slater blue eyes. Except for the shape of their faces and
their smiles, the two twins couldn't look less alike.

"To answer your question, since you didn't come home,
I thought I'd come here."

Josie's gaze went to Vance as he nodded in greeting.
"And you felt the need to bring reinforcements? Hi, Vance.
It's been a long time."

He smiled. "Good to see you again, Josie."

Ana turned back to her sisters. "Vance is here to help
convince you both of the seriousness of the situation." She
wasn't foolish enough to think this would be easy.

Josie's frown told her that she wasn't going to be easily
swayed. "Like I told you when you called last week, I have
a big event coming up. I can't leave right now."

Ana was sad that they wouldn't come back home for
their father. "I understand that, being an event planner, you
need to be here, but I'm talking about our father. We're a
family."

Josie shared a glance with her twin, then said, "It seems
you and Vance have it under control. You two seem to make
a pretty good team. We'll give you permission to make any
decisions. So there's no reason you had to come here and
try and rope us into going back home."

And it wasn't getting any easier, Ana thought. "We came
here because we need to make some decisions about Dad."

"Has something else happened?" Josie asked.

Ana saw the flash of concern and was encouraged. "No, he's the same, and he'll start physical therapy soon."

"That's good, isn't it?" Tori asked.

Good, there was more concern. "The reason we're here isn't so much about Dad as it is about the ranch."

"What do you mean?" Josie asked. "Can't Vance handle things while Colt recovers?"

He gave a nod, but didn't say anything.

"It's more than running the ranch." Ana started to explain, then said, "I wish Marissa was here, too. She should be in on this."

"Maybe I can make it happen," Tori said, and motioned them into her office. Vance, Ana noticed, sat down in the reception area.

Her sister went behind the desk and opened the laptop. "If she's not out on a location, Marissa should be home." After several keystrokes on the computer, a picture came up, then the real thing.

"Hey, Tori."

"Hi, Marissa."

"What's going on?"

"Quite a bit, actually. Got someone here who wants to talk you."

Ana stepped in front of the monitor. She felt tears burning her eyes as her baby sister appeared on the screen, sitting at a desk. "Hi, Marissa."

"Oh, Ana," she sighed. "You're in California?"

She nodded. "I only wish I could see you in person, too. How about I come down to San Diego? If you'll be around."

She saw the panic in her youngest sister's eyes. "Well… maybe, but it's not a good idea right now. I'm going to be out on a shoot all this week. How long are you planning to be here?"

"I need to get back soon to take care of Dad."

Marissa hesitated, then asked, "How is he?"

Ana glanced across the office at Vance, happy for his support. "He's holding his own. That's why I'm here. Uncle Wade came to see me a few days ago. Since Dad is temporarily incapacitated, there needs to be an executor to take over."

"So Uncle Wade is the boss now?"

"No, he isn't. Dad named Vance and me."

The twins shot a look across the office at him. "Why doesn't that surprise me?" Josie said. "He's always treated Vance like family."

Vance didn't say a word for a moment. It was true, Colt had always treated him fairly. Although he wasn't happy about the man's treatment of his daughters.

"Seems I'm the only one who knows about running a ranch," he said eventually.

"That's not our fault," Tori retorted, then all the girls began to argue. That was when Vance put his fingers in his mouth and let go with a loud whistle. It got their attention.

"I didn't ask for the job," he told them. "But since I have it, I'm going to do everything possible to keep the ranch."

Josie looked at Ana. "What does he mean?"

"It means the ranch is in financial trouble. Big trouble." Ana told them about the amount of money owed for the lease, and their six-month extension. "So we need to come up with some ideas."

"Dad doesn't have the money?" Marissa asked.

Ana shook her head, knowing this wasn't going as well as she'd hoped.

"Well, we don't, either," Tori stated. "Everything we have is tied up in the business here."

"It's not only money we want," Vance said. "We need some ideas to add income to the ranch so this doesn't happen again. So tell me, is the Lazy S important enough to you sisters to help save it? Can we count on your support?" After giving them his two cents' worth, Vance turned and walked out of the office.

Tori sighed. "I have to say that cowboy of yours sure knows how to get a woman's attention."

"He's not my cowboy or anything else."

Josie looked at her twin and they both grinned. Then their baby sister's voice said via the computer, "If you say so, sis."

Ana was frustrated, having to defend herself. "I do say so. Vance and I have to work together."

Tori shook her head. "Too bad. You've had that guy tied into knots since you grew breasts."

What? Ana opened her mouth to deny it, but refused to add fuel to the fire. They had other problems. "We need to direct our attention to the ranch."

There was silence and Ana saw the confused looks on her sisters's faces. Of course they were torn. Colt never appreciated anything his daughters had ever done. Tori and Josie had been top students all during school. They'd even won academic scholarships. Marissa had been a star athlete, but over the years their dad had said little in the form of praise or encouragement to any of them. So why should they go back to Montana now?

Ana couldn't make them, but didn't want them to have any regrets, either.

"Okay, sisters," she began. "If you won't do it for our dad, I have another idea." She glanced at the twins, then at Marissa on the computer screen. "Let's do it for ourselves. Let's show Colt Slater how his girls can run the ranch."

CHAPTER FOUR

THREE HOURS LATER, Ana kissed her sisters goodbye and she and Vance left the Slater Style office. She regretted that she hadn't been able to convince them to come home.

She sat in the passenger seat as Vance drove them to the airport hotel. "Go ahead and tell me how badly I handled things."

"No, I'm not saying a thing. Your sisters will have to decide on their own if they want to come home." He stopped at a traffic light, and his dark gaze locked with hers. "I understand how they feel. I've watched for years how Colt treated you girls."

Ana froze. "But you never did anything."

"I can't say I liked it, but I was a kid, too. I liked having a roof over my head, food in my stomach."

Ana remembered the night when Vance had showed up at the supper table, a skinny teenager with a lot of attitude. At first, she felt sorry for him, knowing he had been beaten by his drunken father. Their dad had never laid a hand on them, but it was almost worse when he directed all his positive attention to Vance. It should have come to his daughters.

"We both can agree that Colt never had a sweet disposition," Vance went on. "Truth be known, he doesn't deserve your and your sisters' loyalty. But if I know you girls, you inherited a fair amount of stubbornness and determination from that man. You four aren't about to let the Lazy S fail."

Before Ana could disagree, he pulled up in the circular drive of the large chain hotel. The valet came up to the car and opened her door. "Good evening, ma'am."

She got out and thanked him, while Vance popped the trunk and another attendant helped with the bags.

They arrived at the front desk. A pretty blonde with Jessica printed on her name tag smiled at Vance. Why wouldn't she? He was a handsome man. Dressed in a pair of cowboy boots and creased jeans, he would turn any woman's head. Ana glanced away, hating that she wasn't immune, either.

He placed his hat on the counter. "Hello, ma'am. We need a couple of rooms for tonight."

"Do you have a reservation?"

"I'm sorry, we don't. This was an unexpected trip."

The woman frowned and began to search the computer screen. "We're pretty full tonight."

His dark gaze never wavered as he moved closer. "I'm sure you can find something."

Jessica sighed and went back to her search. "Oh, good. I do have a one-bedroom suite available."

Before Ana could refuse to spend the extra money and the night with this man, Vance said, "We'll take it." He pulled out his credit card, and before Ana recovered, they were riding up in the elevator.

Vance held his breath as they stepped out onto their floor. He was surprised that Ana hadn't fussed about sharing a room. Of course, he hadn't given her much choice. He found their suite and slid the key card into the slot, then pushed open the door and allowed Ana to step in. His body immediately responded to her closeness. He caught her scent as she brushed by him. He sucked in a breath and gave himself a quick talking to, then followed her inside.

The room was fairly spacious. There was a sofa, which was no doubt going to be his bed. He went into the next room to find an inviting king-size bed. *Don't even go there.* He turned and walked away from the temptation.

"You take the bed. I'll sleep out here."

Ana shook her head. "You're too tall for the sofa. You take the bed."

He didn't want to fight about this. "Do you really think you're going to win this argument?"

He could tell she was thinking about it. "Fine. Sleep wherever you want."

What he wanted was not an option. He went to the phone and pressed the button for room service. "What do you want to eat?"

"I don't care." She rolled her suitcase into the bedroom and closed the door.

"It's going to be a long night," he breathed, then said into the phone, "I'd like to order two steaks, medium rare, with baked potatoes and green salad."

They told him thirty minutes. Restless, he went to the mini bar and opened it to find beverages. He bypassed the bottles of beer for a soda. Opening it, he went to the window and drew back the curtains to reveal the millions of lights of Los Angeles. He suddenly missed the isolation of the ranch. Not many lights out there, just millions of stars in the sky.

He turned and found Ana standing across the room. She was still wearing her dark slacks and print blouse, but she was barefoot. "I called the hospital. Dad is resting comfortably. That's a good thing, since he starts therapy tomorrow. I'd like to be there."

"Not sure Colt will be happy about that. I doubt he wants anyone to see him weak."

"Well, he's going to have to get used to it, because he doesn't have a choice."

Vance couldn't help but smile. Ana was definitely her father's daughter.

"I also want to apologize to you."

He liked her being feisty; it helped him keep a safe distance from her. "For what?"

"For arguing about the room. We're both too tired to go looking for another hotel. We're adults and can handle sharing a space for one night."

He nodded, but wasn't so sure. He hadn't been able to spend much time with Ana in the last few years. He'd hoped that would dim his feelings for her. No such luck. He ran his fingers through his hair. "Seems we've been thrown together in an awkward situation. It's been years since we've spent any time together. I can see where you'd feel we're strangers."

She fought a grin. "Yeah, you're the brother I never wanted."

He'd never felt brotherly about her. "Was that why you pretty much hated my guts?"

She frowned. "*Hate* is a strong word. Angry, maybe, because of the attention you got from Dad."

"I wish I could have helped that situation."

Ana shook her head. "No one crossed Colt Slater."

Not true. Vance had one time, when he'd broken that promise to stay away from Colt's daughters. Ana had been the only one who tempted him, that day in the barn when he'd kissed her.

He shook away the memory. "I wish I could have helped, anyway."

A knock sounded on the door. "That's fast." He answered it, expecting supper, but found a bellman with an ice bucket holding a bottle of wine and two glasses.

"Mr. Rivers. Compliments of the management," he said, and waited as Vance stepped aside for him to enter the room. The man set the wine next to the table and began to uncork the bottle. He poured a small amount in a glass and held it out to Vance, who took a taste and nodded. "Very good."

"Thank you, sir. It's from a local winery just north of Los Angeles."

As he filled both glasses, Vance took out some bills and handed them to the waiter, who then left.

"Seems you made an impression on a certain desk clerk," Ana said.

Vance picked up one glass and handed it to her. "Jessica is the assistant manager."

Ana hesitated, but accepted it. "I'm not much of a drinker."

"Nor am I, but I think tonight one glass wouldn't hurt." He raised his glass to her in a toast, then took another drink. "Come see the L.A. stars."

Ana wasn't sure if drinking alcohol was a good idea, but she didn't have to go anywhere. She walked to the big window. "Where?"

He pointed downward. "They're down there. See all the lights."

She smiled, aware of the big man standing very near to her. "Oh, my. That's a lot of houses."

"It looks crowded, too. How do they stand being so close together?"

Ana took another sip, enjoying the taste as the liquid slid down easily. She sipped again and her body began to relax. "And the noise? How do they stand all the noise and traffic?"

He shrugged. "I have no idea. I feel I was pretty lucky to end up at the Lazy S."

"I know." She faced him, feeling overwhelmed by everything that had happened the past week. "I don't want to lose the ranch, Vance. I can't."

He looked down at her. "I promise, Ana. I won't let that happen."

"So you'll help me?"

She realized that his gaze dropped to her mouth. And she suddenly remembered another time when he looked at her that same way. Right before he kissed her. "You don't even have to ask, bright eyes."

His deep, husky voice caused a warm shiver to rush down her spine. She took another sip and suddenly felt light-headed, not knowing if it was the wine or the man. She reached out and touched his forearm to steady herself. Big mistake, looking into his dark eyes. "I like when you call me that." Did she really say that out loud?

Vance frowned. "I think you need to eat something." He took their wineglasses and set them on the table. "Come to think about it, you didn't finish much of your lunch."

Reality came back full force. "Arguing with my sisters always causes me to lose my appetite." She felt the tears welling up. "They are so angry with Dad, but I can't blame them."

He gripped her upper arms. "Look, Ana, you need to give them some time. I have a feeling they'll find their way back home."

She hesitated, so aware of his touch. "Will you leave the ranch if Colt doesn't get better?"

"Do you want me to leave?"

Ana couldn't imagine the Lazy S without him. She shook her head. "No. You have to stay. I mean, you know the operation, the cattle and the crops."

Vance knew that Ana was exhausted. The last few days were beginning to take a toll. Mix in wine and that could mean trouble. What he did like was how agreeable she was with him, and so close. It would be easy to lean down and kiss that tempting mouth of hers.

Whoa. He quickly shook away the thought and stepped back. "Then let's come up with a way to make money."

She picked up her wineglass and took another sip. "What about the roundup?"

"With low cattle prices and our smaller herd, it's not enough. Besides, there's something you girls need to know…." He paused as Ana looked at him with her deep blue eyes. The last thing he wanted to do was give her any more bad news.

"What?"

"It's just that we need more than a temporary fix. Since I've been foreman, the ranch profits have been dwindling. I know there aren't funds to help out with the lean years. We might have to downsize, sell off stock. Norman Stanton would pay dearly for Red Baron."

"Our prize breeding bull?"

Vance nodded. "And there are the horses. Our stallions, Night Ranger and Whiskey King, would bring top dollar."

"Oh, not the horses. Do you really have to sell them off?"

"We might not have a choice. They're a luxury, unless we're going to breed them."

"And sell the foals?"

"That'll take time that we don't have now. We could advertise our studs. It would be more money coming in."

Ana shook her head. "I can't believe that Dad hasn't covered any of our broodmares. Who's the stable manager?"

"You're looking at him. Colt let Charlie Reynolds go last year," Vance told her. "That was a shame, because Charlie had great instincts and was a good trainer. Now our stable is about half of what we once had."

"Did you ask Dad why?"

"Question your father's decision? Not me."

"Something must have happened," she said absently. "It's not like him to be careless about the ranch."

Vance had noticed it, too. "Maybe he wasn't feeling well even then."

Ana didn't like to think her father might have been sick all this time. "Well, he can't tell us now. We just have to find a solution on how to fix it."

A knock sounded on the door. Vance went to let the bellman in with the cart carrying their supper. After being handed the signed receipt, the waiter left.

Vance went back to the table and pulled out Ana's chair. "Let's eat."

She walked over and sat down. "Thank you." She took another sip of her wine and watched as Vance sat down across from her. Yes, the man was handsome. Those deep-set brown eyes, his square jaw covered in a dark shadow from his day's growth of beard. He'd been handsome as a teenager, but as a man he was even more so, being self-assured and confident.

Her focus zoomed in on his mouth. His lower lip was full and had her wondering how it would feel....

She glanced away. What was she doing? She couldn't think this way about Vance Rivers. Not to mention the fact that over the years, he'd had several women on his arm and probably in his bed.

Besides, they had nothing in common but saving the Lazy S. That alone put Vance Rivers way off-limits.

By the time the plane landed the next day, Ana was exhausted from the trip. She hadn't gotten much rest, thanks to the man sleeping just outside her bedroom door.

Vance had parked his pickup at the airport lot before their trip, so they drove straight to the hospital. The ride there was a quiet one, for which Ana was grateful. She had a slight headache, which she contributed to that second glass of wine, one Vance hadn't shared with her.

They got off on the second floor and went directly to Colt's room. There she found the bed empty and her father sitting in a wheelchair.

"Oh, Dad. Look at you." She went to him, and felt the urge to hug him. Instead, she placed her hand on his arm. "How are you feeling?"

Colt only looked at her, then glanced away. Pain shot through Ana's chest. Rejection was something she should be used to, but it still hurt.

A young man wearing dark scrubs walked into the room. He smiled at her. "Well, Colt, seems like you're attracting the ladies today." The man's smile widened as he held out his hand. "Hello, I'm Colt's occupational therapist, Jay McNeal."

Ana shook it. "Ana Slater. Colt's daughter."

Jay glanced down at Colt. "You didn't tell me you had a beautiful daughter."

Ana pulled her hand away. "Has my father had a therapy session yet?"

"Yes, he did," Jay said. "And he did very well."

Vance stood across the room, watching this guy. He never liked his type, always smiling when a woman was around. Vance walked over to Colt and pulled up a chair so he'd be eye level with his mentor-father figure.

"I'm glad to see you up." He glanced at Ana and the therapist as they walked to the other side of the room. "I know this has been rough on you, Colt, but I want you to know that I'm taking care of things at the ranch. I'll hold down the fort until you're well enough to come home."

No response.

Vance decided to try something else to see if he got a response. "Ana and I just got back from Los Angeles. We went to see Tori and Josie, to let them know about your condition."

That did it. Colt shot a look at him and made a groaning sound. Good, a reaction.

"That's right, Colt. Ana is trying to bring them home."

Another groan.

"There's no choice, we need help to run the ranch. Come on, they're your family, and you're lucky to have them." Vance stood and turned toward the door. Stubborn man. Well, Colt needed to get over that real fast.

Frustrated, Colt tried to call Vance back, but he was helpless to speak. Dammit. He couldn't let this happen. His daughters were better off without him. Without a bitter old man who couldn't get over the woman who'd deserted him and their daughters.

From the day their mother left, it had been like that. He knew nothing about raising girls. To make it worse, every time he looked at his beautiful Ana, Tori, Josie and Marissa, all he could see was their mother in their faces. God forgive him, he hadn't been able to get over Luisa's betrayal.

He closed his eyes, wishing for the millionth time that he'd done something that would have changed the past. That he could have gotten his wife to stay, for their daughters at least.

He regretted so many things. The worst had been making his girls suffer because he couldn't deal with his own failure. He glanced down at his useless hand. Now it was too late. He didn't care about the ranch anymore, but he couldn't stand to see the hurt in his daughters' eyes. He'd caused them enough pain. It would be best if they could forget all about him.

The next morning, Ana woke up early and, after Kathleen's insistence on breakfast, drove into town. The first thing she needed was some clothes for her long stay at the ranch.

She stopped at her apartment and packed up her jeans and boots. Suddenly she felt excited that she was going to be living back at the Lazy S for the next few months. She could ride everyday, not just when she could find the time, or figure out when her dad wouldn't be around. She thought about another man who'd be there constantly. Vance. They needed to work together. Not that she had a choice, but this wouldn't be an easy chore. And they still needed to come up with something to help bring in income.

After locking the front door to her one-bedroom apartment, she carried her suitcases to her small SUV. She had two months until her job started back at the high school. If need be she could take off more time, but that was a wait-and-see. They might need her income if the ranch couldn't be saved. Not to mention her father's medical bills.

She shook away that dismal thought and climbed into the car. She drove back through town, down Main Street, passing the many storefronts that made up Royerton. The 1920s buildings housed businesses like the Big Sky Grill, a clothing store, Missy's Boutique, and an antique shop, Treasured Gems. On the corner she saw the familiar brick facade of Clarkson's Trading Post and Outfitters. And smiled, thinking about her close friend Sarah Clarkson. They'd known each other since kindergarten. She was the third generation Clarkson to help run the store.

Ana pulled into a parking space out front and got out. She wanted to thank her friend's family for the flowers and sweet note they'd sent for Colt.

She walked into the shop and was greeted with racks of clothes and walls lined with fishing and hunting equipment. The large store was crowded with customers, this being the height of fly-fishing season. It was a big part of the revenue for the store and the town.

She glanced around and spotted Hank and Beth Clarkson behind the counter, waiting on customers. Sarah had just come out of the back room along with one of the store's licensed outfitters, Buck Patton.

Sarah spotted her and smiled. She held up a finger, asking her to wait, then turned back to the group with Buck and gave instructions. A few minutes later, they all shook hands, before the guide walked the group out the side door to the waiting van.

Sarah rushed over and greeted her with a hug. "Oh, I'm so glad to see you. Is your dad okay? We tried to stop by the hospital but we couldn't see Colt."

Ana nodded. "He's better. He started therapy. I wanted to tell you that I'm moving out to the ranch for the summer."

The pretty redhead blinked at that. "Why? Is your dad coming home so soon?"

Ana shook her head. "No, but I need to help out. It's going to be a long road for Dad's recovery, and since he's incapable of running the ranch right now, I've been named as one of the executors."

"That surprises me. Colt Slater giving anything to his daughters, even responsibility, surprises me."

Sarah knew the history of her family. "Well, I'm not exactly doing this on my own. The other executor is Vance Rivers."

Sarah gasped. "Now, that's no surprise. So are you going to play nice?"

Ana sighed. "We'll be too busy to think about anything

other than running the Lazy S. We have a roundup coming in a few weeks."

Sarah eyed her closely, but before she could make comment, her parents came up to them. They exchanged more
hugs. As a kid, Ana used to wish they were her parents, too.

Beth asked, "How's your Dad, Ana?"

"Better, thank you. He has a long rehab, though."

It was Hank who spoke up. "If anyone can do it, Colt
can. He's too stubborn not to come back from this."

Ana smiled. "He is that."

"You don't need to tell me," Hank said. "For years I've
been trying to get him to allow my outfitters on his land."
The man shook his head. "You have one sweet fishing spot
on the northern section just going to waste."

"You wanted to fish on the ranch?"

Hank nodded. "I wanted to make your dad some money,
too. Colt always said no. He liked his privacy."

Suddenly an idea popped into Ana's head. *Oh, my, could
this work?* "Do you still want to fish on our property?"

Hank paused. "Are you serious? That section of the Big
Hole River is incredible. I could send out day groups. Of
course, the real money is doing overnight trips and week-
ends."

He showed her the chart with the going rates that fishermen paid for these kinds of trips. She nearly fell over.

Ana asked Hank if he could stop by the ranch and they
could go over the section of property in question. When
he agreed, she knew all she needed to do was convince
Vance. Would he go against Colt and side with her? She
shrugged. This was for the sake of the ranch, so they would
deal with the repercussions later.

CHAPTER FIVE

LATER THAT EVENING Vance drove to his house and parked his truck. He'd been at the hospital to see Colt. Not that it had done much good, since the man barely acknowledged his presence. He'd tried to discuss what was going on at the ranch, but Colt seemed disinterested, so Vance had called it a night and left.

On the way back home, he'd stopped by the Big Sky Grill and picked up some dinner. All he wanted tonight was some food and a bed. When he got out of the truck, he heard someone call his name. He turned and saw Ana hurrying along the path from the barn.

His gut tightened as the long-legged brunette headed his way. In his many fantasies, she would be running into his arms, happy that he was home.

She shot him a smile and his pulse began to race. There went his sleep for the night. "What's your hurry?"

"I'm excited," she told him, her breathing a little rough as she held up a manila folder. "You have a few minutes?"

"Sure." He raised his sack. "Mind if we go inside so I can eat my dinner?"

"Oh, sorry. You should eat." She waved at him. "I'll come back."

He reached for her arm to stop her departure. "Don't

go. I mean, it's silly for you to go all the way back to the house. Come inside."

"Only if you eat while I talk."

Together they walked up to the porch. "Sounds like a plan."

Inside, Vance turned on the overhead light and walked to the dining area, put his food sack on the table and his hat on the hook by the back door. "Can I get you something to drink?" He opened the refrigerator. "I have soda and milk."

"Nothing, thank you."

Ana glanced around the room, surprised to see so much detail in the decor. Okay, it was a man's house, but it was clean and organized. The walls were painted a golden hue and the woodwork and trim stained dark. She walked to the large Western painting hanging over the brick fireplace and quickly recognized the signature of a local artist. Then she studied a bronze statue of a horse on the mantel.

"Does it meet with your approval?"

She swung around to Vance. "Sorry, I never thought of you in a house."

He set two soda cans on the table. "Just in a room upstairs in the barn."

She quickly realized how harsh she sounded. "No, I don't see you in the barn. It's just that you have good taste…in decorating." She came back to the table and sat down. "And for the record, Dad should have never let you live in the barn, anyway."

"I think he was trying to protect his four daughters. And it was the apartment over the barn."

Suddenly she was glad for the extra soda, and took a drink. "Please, eat."

Vance sat down across from her in the ladder-back chair. He popped the tab on the can, took a long drink, then unwrapped his meat-loaf dinner from under the foil. "Okay, what's so important you needed to talk about it tonight?"

"Did you know that Dad refused Hank Clarkson's offer of pay to bring fly fishermen on the property?"

With a shrug, Vance scooped up a piece of meat. "A long time ago I heard rumors. I thought it was a friendly disagreement between the two."

She opened the folder. "It's a friendly disagreement that would have brought in a lot of money for the ranch."

Vance continued to eat. "I'm listening."

"Earlier, I drove into town to pick up some clothes from my apartment. Afterward I stopped by Clarkson's Trading Post to see my friend Sarah. Hank Clarkson asked about Dad's condition, then said something about the section of the Big Hole River on our property."

Vance watched as Ana tilted her head, mesmerized by her thick ebony hair brushing against her bare shoulders.

"Seems Hank has several clients who want to fish in a private section of the river." She opened the folder and took out a paper with the going rate anglers pay. "We could be making a portion of that amount."

"Is that before or after the guide and Hank's commission?"

"Well, before, but he's supplying the boats and the guide. It still leaves a lot of money. Hank also said we could make a lot more if he had lodging for overnight trips."

Seeing her excitement, Vance began to realize there could be possibilities, too. "I've fished along the river and the trout are big. It might not be the answer to all of our problems unless…"

Her rich blue eyes lit up and he couldn't look away. "Unless what?"

"A lot of things," he managed to answer. "Do you want

to do this temporarily, or is this going to be a permanent addition to the ranch?"

"Seems that with the ranch having so many bad years, I think we should see where this could take us."

He liked the idea better and better. "Do you want to hire our own guide? Build structures to house the customers?"

She shrugged. "I don't know. What do you think?"

"Shouldn't you talk to your sisters?"

She shook her head. "First, I probably can't get them to make a decision. This is something we can do right now. Hank assured me that he can get some paying customers pronto and I don't want to lose this opportunity." She looked at Vance. "Is it crazy to invest in something like this?"

"Since there isn't a lot of money to spend on investing, maybe we should tread cautiously. See how it works for day fishing first."

"So you like the idea?"

"Yes. It's something that doesn't cost us anything to start with. But we have to do a trial run to see if the investment is worth expanding before we think about building some cabins."

She looked thoughtful. "What about some of our existing buildings? The bunkhouses?"

"They could work, but they'll soon be filled up with the extra hands for the roundup."

She nodded. "Okay, we'll start with day trips. I told Hank that he could stop by tomorrow and check out the best sites. Do you want to come along?"

It would probably be better if he stayed clear of her, but he was pleased that she even asked him. "We're moving the herd down at dawn," he told her. "I guess I could meet you there along the river."

Since the day Vance Rivers had shown up at the Lazy

S, Ana had never wanted to think anything good about him. He'd been the kid who took so much of her father's attention. In all honesty, Vance never had much to do with her dad's decision making. Colt Slater made sure that his word was law. Until now.

She smiled. "Good. I want you there to help in case I have to make any decisions. I don't know the ranch like you do."

"I'm sorry for that."

"It's not your fault, Vance. That was Dad's choice."

"Well, looks like you're involved now. And you have every right to any make decisions about the ranch."

"I'm doing this for all of us." She sighed. "Right now, I'm not sure if my sisters care if the ranch survives or not. But I'm hoping that will change. This is our heritage."

Vance grinned. "Then I guess we better keep the Lazy S going."

Suddenly she felt warm. Undoubtedly, she was attracted to the man, even after all these years. Not a good idea, not when everything depended on them working together.

The next day, Ana had made an early trip to the hospital to see her father. Colt was just as cold and distant as he'd always been. So she left wondering why she even bothered with a man who didn't care.

Glad to be out of the hospital, she checked her watch as she pulled off the highway and onto the river road. It took about ten minutes to get to her destination, where she saw Hank Clarkson walking along the riverbank under the grove of trees. He wasn't alone. The younger, blond man with Hank was Mike Sawhill. She hesitated to get out of her SUV when she recognized him, a man she'd been foolish enough to go out with a few times. When Mike had wanted to push things faster than she wanted to go, things didn't end well.

She climbed out and walked through the high grass to the riverbank, glad she wore her jeans and her cowboy boots. "Hi, Hank." She nodded at the other man. "Mike."

"Hello, Ana. It's been a long time."

She ignored his comment. "Sorry I'm late."

"Not a problem," Hank assured her. "Mike and I were just trying to find the best spot to launch a boat." The older man took off his hat and wiped his brow. "We might need to clear out some brush."

They walked toward the wide river that ran through the Lazy S. She felt the cool breeze off the water, remembering how as kids, she and her sisters would go horseback riding here. They'd strip down to their underwear and get in the cold water.

She brushed aside the fond memory. "Will that be a lot of work?" she asked, trying not to notice that Mike was staring at her.

Suddenly she spotted a horse and rider coming across the pasture. She smiled when she recognized Vance. "Good, he made it."

They all turned as the rider came closer. The man sat in the saddle as if he were born to it. There was an easy familiarity in the way Vance handled the large animal.

He slowed Rusty as he approached them, then walked his mount to the area behind the vehicles and climbed down. After tying the reins to a tree, he strolled over to the group, decked out in working cowboy gear: leather chaps, dusty jeans and boots. Oh my, Vance Rivers looked good.

He pushed his hat back off his forehead. "Sorry I'm late. I had to move a herd." He shook hands with Hank.

"It is roundup time," Hank said, then introduced Mike. "We just got here ourselves."

Ana watched something flash between the two men, and stepped in. "Did everything go okay?"

"Yeah, just had to chase down a lot of strays." He smiled at her. "What did I miss?"

"Hank's a little worried about the steep bank and brush, for launching a boat from here."

Vance caught Mike Sawhill's close attention on Ana. He didn't like it. "There might be a better spot about a quarter mile downstream. I've caught my share of browns and rainbows there."

They took off and walked the distance. After being in the saddle all morning, Vance didn't mind stretching his legs. In between answering questions from Hank, he also watched Ana's uneasiness around Mike.

Vance didn't know the angler guide personally, but he'd seen him around town, especially in Montana Mick's Bar, usually with a lady.

He suddenly felt protective, and called to Ana. She turned around, and he asked about her visit with Colt. It distracted her from whatever Sawhill was saying to her.

They finally reached their destination. "Here it is," Vance announced as they turned toward the bank. The area was shaded by leafy trees, and the bank wasn't as steep and had a small clearing.

"I've fished here a few times, but never launched a boat. So you'll have to tell me if it will work."

The two men went to examine the bank closer, giving Vance a chance to talk to Ana. "Is Sawhill someone to you?"

She glared at him. "No!" she muttered, keeping her voice down.

Vance could see there had been some history between them. He didn't like that, not at all.

When the two men walked back, Hank was smiling.

"It's a great spot. There's plenty of shade and the water is deep." He looked at Ana. "How soon do you want your first customers?"

Ana glanced at Vance, then back at Hank. "Is there anything we need to do to get ready?"

"Not to begin with. I have several locals who've been itchin' to cast a fly in this section of the river. No angler wants to compete in a crowd." Hank looked at Mike. "Day after tomorrow?"

Mike nodded. "I have a group of four. We'll be testing the water to see what we catch. Thing is, the Big Hole River is all good."

Hank smiled again. "Is that okay with you?" he asked Ana.

Her eyes widened. "Sure."

The older man shook his head. "Relax, Ana. We're doing all the work. Now, if you had lodging, there's a group coming in this weekend. I'll have to put them up in the local motel."

Vance was suddenly curious. "How many anglers, and what do they expect in accommodations?"

"It's a group of four who are pretty easy to please. A roof over their heads and a bed. A bonus would be to not have to cook."

Vance glanced at Ana, then said, "I've got a house at the ranch, and if Kathleen will cook a little extra, we can throw in a few meals, too."

Ana shook her head. "No, Vance. You can't give up your place."

He shrugged. "Not a problem." He shot a look at Mike. "I'll just move up to the main house with you."

"I can't believe you said that," Ana said as she marched up to Rusty's stall an hour later. She was not happy with Vance.

She leaned against the wooden slats as he began to brush the animal.

"I don't see the problem," he told her. "It's my house to give up."

"You know that's not what I'm talking about. You made them think that there's something going on between us."

"Can I help what they think?"

"You can when you direct them there," she countered.

"Okay, you're right, but I didn't like the way Sawhill was looking at you. And admit it, you're uncomfortable around him."

"I can handle any problem with Mike."

Vance paused in grooming Rusty. "So you admit there's a problem."

"Look, we only went out a few times. I didn't feel anything for the guy so I didn't continue seeing him. He didn't like that."

"Did he bother you today?"

"No. So I don't need you to intervene. But now you made it so people think I'm…"

"Involved with that wild Rivers kid," he finished for her.

"I didn't mean it like that." She released a sigh. "Don't we have enough to do without adding to it?"

"I don't see I'm adding to anything. I solved a couple of problems. One, I got Sawhill off your back, stopped him thinking about trying to start up something again."

"I'm not interested, anyway." This man was infuriating. "It was only a few dates, a few kisses," she said, lowering her voice, wanting to walk away. She wasn't going to discuss another man with him.

Vance put away the brush. "Secondly, we have paying customers, and add in lodging, there's a lot more money coming in. Say, 'thank you, Vance.'"

Ana knew she was being stubborn about this. Why did

she have a problem with him staying in the house? Maybe because there were just the two of them, and with the attraction she was feeling, it wasn't safe. "Okay, thank you."

Vance stroked Rusty across his back, then walked out of the stall. "It's only for a week, Ana. Could you put up with me that long?"

They started down the barn aisle. At this time of day the men were out doing chores. So besides the horses in their stalls, they were pretty much alone.

"Or should I move back into my old room in the barn, or the bunkhouse?"

She stopped. "I can't let you do that. Of course you can move into the house."

Vance's eyes softened, then he gripped her hand and pulled her into the empty corner stall.

"Vance, what are you doing?"

With a tug of her hand, he had her suddenly against his body. "I thought since you don't want to be seen with me, we shouldn't let anyone see when I do this." His mouth closed over hers, and Ana wanted to cry out for him to stop, but that would be a lie. She'd wanted this since Los Angeles. His mouth slanted over hers and her arms wrapped around his neck as the kiss deepened.

A soft moan escaped her lips as she moved closer, so close she could feel the hard planes of his chest. Oh, God. Her body was betraying her as she eagerly returned his kiss.

He finally broke away and looked down at her. His dark gaze was heated. "It seems your kissing has improved over the years."

The room was dark, as much as a hospital room could be. Colt couldn't wait to get out of this place. To be able to sleep in his own bed, in his own house. He closed his eyes and realized that might never happen.

If he didn't get better, he couldn't go back to the ranch—that was a fact. So he needed to get his strength back, to relearn to walk and talk again. It had been barely a week since his stroke, since his entire life fell apart.

God, he was only fifty-four years old. What had happened? Lousy habits for one, along with stress and endless hours of work. That wasn't any kind of life. He thought back over years of not caring about anything. He'd lost so much, he hadn't wanted to go on, especially after the girls left home. Hell, he'd driven them away, and ended up all by himself. Vance was the only one who'd hung in with him and the ranch. Now Colt was pretty sure he would lose the Lazy S and rot away in some nursing home.

He thought back to the early years and the joy he once had in his life. Luisa and their beautiful daughters. They were all gone, except for Ana. For some crazy reason she wanted him to survive. He felt a surge of hope. Maybe he could salvage something and at least have part of a family.

He needed to get better. He glanced down at his lifeless hand and recalled what his therapist, Jay, had said: "You have to put in the time and hard work."

Colt stared down at his hand again, willing it to move. It seemed to take forever, but he finally lifted two of his fingers. Then he dropped his head back on the pillow and smiled, feeling for the first time in a long time that he wanted to do this. He thought back to his rodeo days and the determination it took to climb on a bull, to ride the eight seconds.

Colt opened his mouth, working to form something more than a grunt. "Sss…second ch…chance," he said in the silent room.

The small accomplishment brought more joy than he'd

felt in years. Suddenly, he didn't want to just lie down and die. There were things he needed to change and correct before he checked out of this world.

He closed his eyes, and this time sleep finally came, but so did a dream of his beautiful Luisa.

She stood in the doorway, then it seemed she floated across the room to his bedside. She leaned in closer and he could see her face, her beautiful face.

"Colton," she whispered.

Her voice touched off so many feelings, feelings he'd suppressed for years since she had abandoned him. Yet the pull was too strong to deny. "Luisa." He tried to open his eyes, but couldn't. "Luisa."

"I'm here, Colton." She touched his face. "I've always been here."

CHAPTER SIX

"I'M SO SORRY, ANA," Sarah said as they sat at a corner table in the Big Sky Grill the next day. "I had no idea Mike was the guide going with Dad yesterday."

"It's not a problem," Ana told her friend. "It's not like I'm going fishing with the group. So we won't cross paths again."

Sarah munched on a French fry, then said, "Mike can be a pain in the butt sometimes with his flirting, but he knows if he steps over the line he'll have to deal with Dad." She leaned back in her seat. "And he likes his job too much for that."

Ana had always envied her friend's relationship with her father, their closeness. "It wasn't a problem. I can handle Mike."

Sarah leaned forward and lowered her voice. "And it didn't hurt to have Vance Rivers come to your rescue."

Not hungry any longer, Ana pushed her club sandwich away. "I didn't need to be rescued at all." She shook her head. "What is it about men that makes them think they need to compete against each other, and I'm the prize?"

Sarah smiled. "I'd say you're a pretty lucky girl. I wouldn't mind having someone like Vance around...just in case."

Ana tried not to think about him that way. "Sarah, you know we have to work together. That's all that's going on."

"So you don't have any feelings for the man? No sparks between you two?"

Ana shook her head, knowing she was lying. Yesterday's kiss in the barn proved that there were sparks. Okay, more like fireworks. But what about Vance? Was he trying to prove a point by kissing the boss's daughter, as he had all those years ago?

Sarah's voice quickly brought Ana back to reality. "I would think a man as handsome as Vance would get your juices flowing."

"I can't afford to get anything flowing. We have to focus on the ranch. And there's Dad to think about. I have too much on my plate right now to think about him or any man."

"I'm sorry, Ana. Is there anything I can do to help?"

"You're a good friend, Sarah. Thank you, but unless you want to drag my sisters back here, there isn't much you can do." She smiled. "Taking me to lunch was the best. Thanks for calling and insisting I come into town."

"A lot of good it did." She nodded to the nearly untouched sandwich. "You aren't eating enough."

Ana sighed. "I'm not very hungry."

"Well, make yourself eat. Colt needs you to stay strong."

Did her father even care? She knew that he needed her at the ranch. Whether he wanted her there or not, she wasn't sure. But she wanted him well and back home to run the Lazy S. Then she could go back to her life. Her job. Except for the kids at the school, there was no one special waiting for her.

The following morning came far too soon for Ana. She got up with the sun, ate toast for breakfast and drank down some coffee, then headed out to the barn. She was going to do whatever needed to be done.

She was ready to face Vance, whom she hadn't seen in two days. Once inside the barn, she found a list of chores hanging on the door of the tack room, but no Vance around. The note stated that he'd gone out with most of the ranch hands, who were moving the herd.

She shook off her disappointment that she hadn't been asked to go along, then went to start her tasks. At the feed bin, she began to scoop out the morning's rations of oats for the horses. With Jake's help she got the job done within the hour. Then the cleaning began, the mucking out stalls and hosing down the center aisle.

She even had the buckskin, Blondie, in the washing area. By the time she was finished with the bathing, she was as wet as the horse.

It felt good to do physical labor. It took her mind off everything except the job at hand. She walked Blondie back to her clean stall. The horse nudged her for more attention.

"If I have time later, it's you and me headed across the meadow." She gave the affectionate horse one more rub and left the stall.

Jake walked by, whistling. "Thanks for the help, Ana."

"Not a problem. What's next?"

The twenty-one-year-old smiled. "We're finished for the morning."

"Good, then I think I'll go up to shower." Ana wrinkled her nose. "I can't stand myself any longer."

She took off toward the house, then paused to admire the huge stone and brown-clapboard structure. The original two-story house had been built for her mother, but over the years, they'd added on as each baby came along. Now it looked big and empty and in need of some tender loving care.

Ana walked up the stone path to the back door, to find Kathleen folding clothes in the utility room.

"Hold it right there, young lady. You're not going into the house wearing those filthy clothes." The housekeeper handed her a towel from a stack of clean ones. "Strip and put everything in the hamper." She shook her head. "This sure brings back memories. You always could get the dirtiest of all your sisters. I miss those times," she said, lifting a basket of clean clothes and walking out.

Ana smiled as she kicked off her boots and unzipped her jeans, shimmied the wet fabric down her legs and tossed them into a hamper. That was the benefit of staying for the summer: she got to be around the horses and live here at the ranch. She pulled off her sweatshirt and threw it on top of the jeans. She was shivering by the time she got out of her soggy panties and bra. She reached for the towel and wrapped it around her just as the back door opened.

Ana gasped in shock when she turned around and saw Vance step into the small room.

"What are you doing here?" she demanded, gripping her towel tightly.

He didn't answer right away, but his gaze took a slow journey up her body. "Right now, I'm enjoying the view."

She felt warmth surge through her. "Well, stop it."

He tipped his hat back and leaned against the doorjamb. "That's a little hard to do." He shook his head. "Damn, if you don't look good in a towel."

"Oh, grow up." She hated that he made her feel so anxious. "I'm going to take a shower. So if you need anything… I mean, is there something I can do—"

"Believe me, a lot is coming to mind, but right now I just need to move in." He grinned. "Looks like I'm going to be enjoying my stay here."

Ana didn't have a comeback, so she swung around and

marched off with as much dignity as she could manage in a towel. All the way reminding herself that there would be a man in the house. A man she definitely needed to stay clear of.

Vance enjoyed the view from the back almost as much as the front. But if he wasn't careful, and if he came on too strong, Ana would run far and fast. He frowned. The wise thing to do might be to back off completely, as he'd been doing for years. Yet all he could think about was the kiss they'd shared in the barn. No other woman could tie him in knots like Analeigh Slater.

Hell, he'd thought the years apart would lessen his appetite for the pretty brunette. But all she had to do was flash those big blue eyes at him, and once again he couldn't remember his name.

He grabbed the duffel bag outside the door and walked into the kitchen just as Kathleen was coming down the hall.

She gave him a bright smile. "So now I know what's got my girl so riled up." The housekeeper paused. "A word of advice, Vance. Don't push too hard."

He played innocent. "I only came by to drop off some things in my room."

The older woman shook her head. "Yeah, I know. Just be warned, Ana is vulnerable right now. She's been fighting for her daddy's approval all her life." Kathleen pushed her finger into his chest. "I don't think you'd ever break her heart intentionally, but…just tread softly."

Vance felt his chest tighten. That would be the last thing he would ever do. He was more worried that she would destroy him.

An hour later, Ana came out of the same bedroom she'd slept in since she was a little girl. She was freshly showered and shampooed, realizing she'd be sharing a bath with Vance at least for a few days.

In the past four years, she'd seen Vance Rivers only in town. They would nod in greeting, but rarely exchanged words. Now she had to work with the man, and she'd be sleeping a few doors down the hall.

Okay, it was a big house. There were four bedrooms upstairs and a master suite at the opposite end. They could go their separate ways, except when they needed to come up with ideas to help the ranch.

She headed for the stairs and saw her sister Marissa's bedroom door was open. There was Vance, taking clothes out of his bags and putting them in the dresser drawers.

In the walk-in closet there was a row of shirts hanging neatly. Well, he was making himself at home. Ana closed her eyes. He had every right to be here. He'd been a part of this family for years. He should be like a brother to her. So why didn't she feel sisterly toward him?

Just then Vance turned around, and she zoned in on the tall, broad-shouldered man with that lanky cowboy build a woman couldn't take her eyes off. Her gaze moved to his handsome face with those deep-set, coffee-colored eyes. His sandy-brown hair was thick and wavy, and maybe a little on the long side.

"See anything you like?" he asked.

"Well, you were checking me out downstairs. I thought I'd turn the tables and see how you like it."

He dropped his stack of T-shirts and came toward her. "I like it a lot, especially from you," he told her.

She fought to move away, but he was so close, and so tempting. "This playing around isn't a good idea, Vance."

"Who said I was playing?" he challenged.

Her heart started to pound as she met his intense gaze.

She managed to step back. "Whatever it is, stop it. We need to concentrate on other things. Are you settled in?"

"I'm getting there. Back at my house, I put away all my personal things. Jake and Gary moved beds from the bunkhouse into the other two bedrooms. So the place now sleeps four to five adults. Kathleen is going to put on the bedding and add some special touches."

"Thank you, Vance. Thank you for doing this."

"It's not a big deal. The house is part of the ranch. It's not even mine."

"But it comes with your job as foreman."

Vance had plans to have his own place soon. The dream might be pushed further into the future than he wanted, but he wasn't giving up. He had the land, and the crop nearly ready to harvest, and soon he'd be able to build his house. He looked at Ana. Question was, would he ever have the girl?

"I can handle living here," he said, wanting to change the subject. "I bet your sister would have a fit knowing I'm sleeping in her room."

Yeah, and so close to me. Ana suddenly remembered the kid who used to sleep in the barn.

"Like I said before, Colt should have never made you stay out in the barn," she said.

Vance raised an eyebrow. "He didn't make me stay any-where."

"A boy shouldn't have to live with animals."

"It wasn't that bad. Really. My room was upstairs. It was a big area, and finished just like a regular house."

"But you were a kid," she insisted. "You needed adult supervision."

"I was fourteen," he told her. "Chet was close by. I had pretty much been living on my own for years. Though my mother left, my dad was around most of the time. I liked being at the ranch, because he wasn't there taking a swing at me." Vance glanced away. "It was heaven to have a warm bed, three square meals and clothes."

Ana felt the tears building.

He gave a frustrated sigh. "Don't you do that! Don't go feeling sorry for me. I've had a good life here. Your father took me in, helped me learn about horses and cattle. He gave me a chance at a good life, Ana. So just drop this."

Seeing her frown, he quickly changed to another topic. "I heard you worked pretty hard today."

"Isn't that what you wanted? There was a list."

He folded his arms over his chest. "I post a list every day, but I didn't expect you to do it all."

"I want to help out."

"You don't need to go overboard, Ana. There are men who get paid to do the job."

"You can't expect me to sit around and do nothing."

He hesitated. "Then how about taking a ride with me this afternoon? I need to help with the herd."

She was excited. "You're not just making the trip up for me?"

He shook his head. "I don't have time for that. I wouldn't have come in, except I needed to get my clothes out of the house. I'd planned to go back out after lunch. You can come along or not." He went back to putting clothes away in the dresser.

"I'll come," she agreed.

"Then let's have some lunch and go."

She smiled, and he found there was nothing sweeter.

There was nothing like the view of the mountains and feeling the cool breeze against her cheeks as she raced across the pasture. Blondie loved to run, so Ana gripped the horse's mane and let her have her lead through the high grass.

She glanced over her shoulder and saw Vance on Rusty only a slight distance behind her. He could easily catch her, but she was glad he allowed her the freedom to do her thing.

Finally, he rode up beside her and pointed toward the pasture, where cattle dotted the landscape.

"Fun is over, it's time to go to work," he called to her.

Ana pulled back on the reins and her mount slowed. They approached the herd of Hereford cows with their babies, and she immediately heard the calves bawling. She smiled at the familiar sound, and inhaled the scents of cattle and fresh grass.

Vance closed the space between them. "You ride in with the herd. I need to check for strays."

With her nod, Vance kicked Rusty's sides and they took off after an errant yearling. Ana couldn't help but smile, seeing the gelding react like a pro cutting horse. She knew Vance had entered Rusty in many competitions.

The horse and rider were putting on a show now. They headed off the calf, and a dance of wills began between the equine and cow, until Vance managed to direct the little guy back to the herd and his mama.

Ana walked Blondie along with the herd, careful not to startle any of the cows. Vance soon fell in beside her.

"Pretty impressive work."

"Thank you, ma'am." He tapped the brim of his hat with a gloved finger. "You want to play cowgirl?"

She nodded. "Show me what to do."

"Watch Gary and Todd," he told her.

She leaned over her saddle horn and spotted two young cowboys with lariats in their hands, using the ropes to keep the cows in a tight group. Before she could ask, Vance handed her a bandanna from his pocket.

"Tie this around your mouth. It keeps out the dust."

She did as he told her, then he handed her a rope and rode with her to the back of the herd. "We're going to ride drag, but the dust shouldn't be too bad, since it rained last night."

"It's okay," she said. "Where are we taking them?"

"A good mile to the branding pens." He looked concerned. "Will you be okay?"

She nodded, though she wasn't sure. "I can do this."

He winked at her. "I don't doubt you can." He stayed with her, sending Gary and Todd to flank the herd, and they continued the slow process of moving the cows.

Nearly two hours later, they finally reached the large pens. They got the herd through the gate, where Gary had feed waiting for the hungry cows. Once the last one was inside and the gate shut, Ana climbed down from her horse.

"Oh," she cried, as her legs started to give way, but she felt someone grip her by the waist and hold her upright.

"Whoa, there," Vance said against her ear.

"I'm okay." She held on to the saddle horn, hoping he'd release her.

"You sure?"

"Let go and find out."

He did. And by a miracle, she managed to stay on her tired legs. "I guess I'll need to toughen up."

"Not too much." He tossed her a wide grin. "I kind of like your soft places."

Before she could say anything, he walked off to help the men. She decided that she would stay and rest a minute or two, or a hundred. Oh, boy. She moved very gingerly to the shade of a tree and leaned against the trunk. How would she pull this off tomorrow?

She smiled. She didn't care. All the aches and pains were so worth it. For once she felt she was a part of this ranch, and decided she was going to find a way to stay and be a part of this operation. She looked at Vance walking to his horse. He wore leather chaps over his jeans and a cowboy hat low on his head.

The man took charge as if he were born to the job. Well, so was she. She just needed a little practice at being a cowgirl, and couldn't let one good-looking cowboy distract her.

By the time they got back from the cattle pens, they were both exhausted and dirty. After taking care of the horses, Vance went into the bunkhouse for a shower, leaving Ana a chance for some privacy. Not that he wanted to be apart from her. He'd enjoyed spending the day with her, and wouldn't mind more.

He stripped down and walked into the large shower stall. He closed his eyes as the warm spray hit his tired body, but he wasn't too tired to think about Ana. The picture of her standing naked in the big tub at the house flashed into his head. Water would be slicing over her slender frame from the overhead spray, her soapy hands moving over those sweet curves. His mouth went dry as he remembered the taste of her mouth, and he ached to sample the rest of her.

With a frustrated groan, he reached out and turned the faucet to cold, and quickly finished washing. He got out, dried off and wrapped himself in a towel. He cursed, knowing Colt would have a fit if he knew Vance had been thinking this way about his oldest daughter.

He walked out of the shower area, stood at the mirror over the row of sinks and ran his hand over his two-day growth of beard. He'd no sooner reached inside his shaving kit for his razor when he heard a gasp.

He glanced in the mirror and saw Ana standing in the doorway.

What the hell… "Ana. Is something wrong?"

Looking embarrassed, she shook her head. "Jake told me… He said that there was some liniment…in here." She shuddered. "He said it would help with my soreness."

Vance glanced over her long legs encased in a clean pair of jeans. By the looks of her still-damp hair she'd already showered.

"Your legs hurt?"

"Along with other body parts," she murmured.

He tried not to think about the parts she didn't mention. It didn't work.

"I want to be able to help with the branding tomorrow, so I need to do something to help my aches and pain."

She was staring at him as if she'd never seen a man in a towel before. He liked the interest he saw in her eyes. As much as he wanted to see where this would go between them, this wasn't the time.

"Maybe you should just take a day or two off," he suggested.

She frowned. "But I want to help."

"You don't need to prove anything, Ana." He opened the counter drawer, searched around and found a tube of ointment. He held it up. "You're already sore from today's ride."

She straightened, then crossed the room and took the tube from him. "Then let me prove it to myself. I can handle tomorrow."

He gripped her by the wrist. "I just don't want you to get hurt in the process."

She looked both sad and angry. "So you expect me to just stand around?"

"I want you safe. Those calves can be downright ornery

when they're riled." He stepped closer, reached out and touched her cheek. "I don't want this pretty skin bruised."

He saw the pulse pounding in her neck, and her breathing changed, too. "Vance…"

He looked into her deep blue eyes and a sudden jolt rocked his gut. He wanted this woman. "Damn, Ana, what you do to me."

She started to glance away, but his touch drew her back as he lowered his head and brushed his mouth across hers. She drew in a sharp breath, but he didn't stop, just went back again. He teased her lower lip, then moved to kiss the corners of her mouth. But before he could get seriously into her, the sound of voices drew them apart.

He cursed and she jumped back. "I've got to go."

She hurried out of the bathroom, leaving him aching for what he wanted but might never have. Yet he couldn't give up on this chance. He only needed to convince Ana.

CHAPTER SEVEN

THAT NIGHT, DINNER was quiet. Ana attributed it to being tired from the long day. And the kiss. What did she say to the man when he acted as if it had never happened?

She thought of her invasion of his privacy in the bunk-house shower. He'd been practically naked. Okay, he had on a towel, but his muscular chest and wide shoulders were exposed for the world to see. So she'd stood there ogling him like a silly teenager. Not that it had bothered him at all. The big mistake was when she let him kiss her. Again. What was it about this man that drew her? That made her so aware that she was a woman?

She glanced at Vance. He was sitting in the same seat he'd been assigned when he first came here to live. Right next to Colt. She also remembered how right after the meal was finished Vance would carry his plate to the kitchen, then go back to his room…in the barn. He had never been allowed to join in anything with her and her sisters.

And from the minute the young, moody Vance set foot on the ranch, Ana had been aware of him. As a preteen girl she'd thought it was just an annoyance and would go away when he left. But Vance never left the ranch, and for a long time she'd blamed him for taking Colt from his family.

Once in college, she'd met and gotten engaged to Seth. Things should have been perfect, but then he'd wanted to move to a larger city. Despite Colt's rejection, she wanted to live close to home, to her sisters, even her dad…and Vance?

He glanced up. "I can hear you thinking."

"What?" she said too loudly, then lowered her voice even though they were alone. Kathleen had gone to play her weekly bingo game. "I'm just tired." Ana pushed her plate away.

He tossed her a grin. "Or maybe you're thinking about earlier. It's nice to know that you were affected by the kiss."

She worked at slowing her breathing and heart rate. "It was barely a kiss."

"Give me more time and you won't have any doubts."

She raised her hand. "No. Not a good idea."

He hesitated, not looking happy. "You're right. We've been denying this between us for years, so why not continue?"

Was she ready to face this? No. "Just because there's an attraction between us doesn't mean we should act on it."

"Right again." He slid his chair back and stood. "I'm needed in the barn."

"Vance," she called.

He stopped and turned around. "If I don't leave now, Ana, I'm going to do my damnedest to prove you wrong." His dark eyes bored into hers. "You ready for that?"

She hesitated, feeling the heat from his gaze. Was she ready for this? She did the safe thing and shook her head.

He turned and walked out.

The next day, Colt listened as Dr. Mason went over his progress with Ana. He liked what he heard, except for the part that said he needed to go to a rehab facility to finish his therapy.

Great. He was headed for the nursing home to be left

to rot. He glanced at Ana and saw the concern etched on her face.

"Why can't Dad come home?" she asked.

Dad. She'd always called him Colt. He felt his chest tighten and his eyes water.

Ana looked at him and smiled. "Why couldn't we just have an occupational therapist come to the ranch?"

The neurologist shook his head. "He'll need a full-time nurse along with a therapist. And unless you're independently wealthy, that's expensive. The insurance companies don't pay for full-time in-home care."

"I didn't know." Ana was silent a moment, then said, "So going into the rehab center is the best option?"

Madison nodded. "And Jay McNeal will still be working with him."

Ana turned back to Colt and touched his arm. "Would you like that, Dad? For Jay to keep working with you?"

Hell, the guy was tough as nails, but Colt didn't want him to back down. With a groan, he nodded, and was rewarded with another smile. Her pretty face lit up. Suddenly, Luisa came to mind. No. He wouldn't let that woman get to him ever again. She'd already helped destroy his relationship with his daughters. No, that was the one thing he couldn't blame on his ex-wife. He had done that all by himself.

The doctor and Ana walked across the room to where Vance stood. Colt noticed that Vance couldn't take his eyes off her. There was no doubt about the desire burning in the kid's eyes. This time it looked as if Colt was going to lose Analeigh to another man.

Two mornings later Vance was up before dawn. He had a date with about a hundred calves that needed to be branded and castrated before they were hauled off to the feedlot. He climbed out of bed and slipped on his jeans and shirt.

He'd had a lousy night's sleep. *Thank you, Ana.* But he knew he'd created his own problem and had to deal with it. He needed to stay away from the temptation. Not a problem. They had the roundup the next two days, and with the anglers arriving this morning to stay at his house, that should be plenty to keep him distracted.

Sitting on the edge of the bed, he grabbed a pair of socks and worked them on, then stuck his foot into the boot shaft and tugged his jeans down over the decorative stitching. He stood and ran his fingers through his hair, then made a quick stop in the bathroom.

He'd just stepped into the hall when Ana's bedroom door opened and she appeared in a skimpy pair of boxer shorts and a tank top. *Whoa, dogie.* His body immediately reacted, making it difficult to speak.

"Vance." She said his name in a low, sleep-laced voice. That didn't help the situation.

"Why didn't you wake me?" she asked.

He swallowed, knowing that would have made matters worse. "I was going to, but thought you could use a little more sleep and head out later."

She nodded. "Just give me two minutes and I'll be ready."

He was hoping for a different answer. "The anglers are coming today," he called. "Wouldn't you like to stay around and greet them?" Truth was, he didn't want her getting hurt, or worse, distracting him.

"Hank's taking them fishing first thing this morning. I'll welcome them tonight." She disappeared back into the bedroom, leaving the door partly open, so he saw her shirt go flying, along with her boxers. Great. He was supposed to sit in a saddle all day with the picture of a naked Ana in his head?

A minute later the door swung open and she came out dressed in jeans and socks, buttoning her blouse over a tank top. She ran across the hall into the bathroom and shut the door. Vance leaned against the wall, wondering if he should go on ahead, but seconds later she walked out, grabbed her jean jacket and began to tie her hair back. "I'm ready."

He liked her fresh look—no makeup, not fussing with her hair. "We'll grab some breakfast at the bunkhouse."

She smiled and reached for her boots at the back door. Sitting down, she worked the scuffed buckskins on, then grabbed an old cowboy hat off the hook and headed with him toward the barn. Suddenly, he was looking forward to spending the day with her.

When they arrived, they found Jake loading up the truck. "Is there any food left?" Vance asked.

"Sure." The kid nodded. "Morning, Ana."

"Good morning, Jake."

They kept on walking to the bunkhouse. They heard the men talking, and some were joking around, but when Ana stepped through the door, silence blanketed the room.

"Hey, don't stop on my account," she said.

Todd got up and motioned to her to take the spot. "We were just sayin' how this roundup won't be the same without Colt."

Vance caught Ana's sadness. "You know he wishes he could be here," she told them. "With the way the rehab is going, I'm sure he'll make the next one. So you guys will just have to put up with me today."

Pete Cochran stood. "I'll say you're a lot better looking than old Colt. Your daddy would be proud of you, Ana."

She blushed as he handed her a plate. "You'd better eat. You've got to show these guys you're a Slater."

By noon, Ana was tired and smelled of sweat, dirt and cows, but had never felt better. She couldn't work as hard as the men, but she'd done her share.

She stood at the pen gate and watched as the roper, Todd, lassoed another calf and dragged him over to the branding area, where Vance wrestled him to the ground. Next the heeler held down the hind legs as Pete did the quick job of castrating the calf.

"Okay, let's brand this guy," Vance called.

Ana went into motion, hurrying out with the iron and pressing it against the calf's hind quarter. The smell of burning cowhide filled the air as the Slater brand was engraved onto the animal. She pulled the iron away and saw the sign for the lazy S.

"Next," she called, as they released the animal and he ran off to his mama.

"Good job."

She looked at Vance, feeling a sense of pride for what she was accomplishing and for the generations of Slaters who'd come before her. "Thanks."

She stood back and watched the men work together. She knew she got the honor of branding only because of Vance, but she'd take it.

Suddenly, the sound of the dinner bell rang out. "Lunch break," Kathleen called.

They turned around and found that the housekeeper and some of the men had set up tables under a group of huge oak trees.

The ranch hands started walking over, eager for some of Kathleen's famous fried chicken and rice and beans.

There were several salads to choose from, so something had to be to their liking.

Ana smiled when she arrived to wash up. Once her hands were clean she got in the food line.

"Land's sake, child," Kathleen called to her. "Have you been playing in the dirt?"

Grinning, Ana looked down at her mud-spattered jeans and boots. "You could say that," she agreed as she moved on with her heaping plate. She walked toward the shady area and spotted two high school students, Billy Kramer and Justin Patchett. She stopped and talked with them, then moved on past another table. She recognized a few of their neighbors and thanked them for helping out. One in particular, who was seated at the end, she hadn't seen in years—Garrett Temple. The tall, dark-haired man had been their closest neighbor, and according to Colt, their biggest enemy.

"Garrett."

He raised his head and his smile died as he slowly rose to his feet. "Hello, Ana. It's been a long time."

"Yes, it has. Are you helping with the roundup?"

He nodded. "If this isn't a good idea, I'll leave."

She recalled that Colt and Garrett's father, Nolan, had had a feud going for years. So had Garrett and Josie, but theirs was a more personal one. Ana hadn't been happy about the way Garrett treated her sister, but that had been years ago, back in their first years of college.

"Why would I want that?"

With that, Garrett smiled. "Considering our families' history, I don't want to cause any trouble."

She didn't want to rehash anything from the past. "Colt isn't here."

"I know. I'm sorry to hear about his stroke. Vance said he's doing well."

It was nice that Garrett asked. "He's going through rehab now. We're hoping to have him home soon."

"That's good to hear."

Ana smiled, then said, "Maybe for you, but Colt isn't the easiest man to deal with, and trying to keep him down during his recovery will be nearly impossible."

Garrett laughed at that. "I know. My dad is just as stubborn."

Vance heard Ana's laugh and turned around to see her with Garrett. A funny feeling came over him when he saw how she was looking up at his friend. Her eyes sparkled, as if she was hanging on his every word.

"Hey, boss." Todd walked over and asked him a question about the afternoon crew.

By the time Vance looked back at the couple, he found that Ana had sat down at the table with Garrett. No, he didn't like this one bit.

He grabbed a plate, filled it and made his way over to the table just as the pair looked up.

"Hey, Vance, sit down," Garrett said. "Ana and I were just catching up about the kids we knew."

Well, that was one conversation he couldn't join in. "That's good."

Garrett grinned. "Can you believe that she's working at the high school?" He turned back to Ana. "Do the students give you as hard a time as we gave the teachers?"

"Some of them do, but for the most part, they're pretty good kids."

Vance concentrated on eating, but his food was suddenly tasteless. He had nothing in common with Ana or Garrett. He'd been ahead of them in school, and they hadn't run in the same social circles.

The reminiscing continued between the two until Vance

couldn't take any more. He stood, and Garrett looked at him. "You're leaving?"

"Some of us have to work." He walked off, knowing he was acting like a jerk. But that didn't seem to stop him.

Okay, so this place might not be so bad.

Colt looked around the rehab facility's community room with its large, flat-screen television and several card tables set up for socializing. His bedroom wasn't so bad, either. He'd been here only a few days, so he'd reserve judgment on how he felt about the place.

He did like having familiar faces around. And Jay made sure he was working hard on his exercises, even had him up and walking with the help of the parallel bar today. Colt also had a speech therapist now. It was a little crazy to start making sounds as if he were a baby, but it seemed to help him.

He just wished someone could help ease his frustration. No one would tell him how much this was costing, or how long he'd be staying here. All he knew was he couldn't afford it if he had to pay. He might as well sign over the Lazy S, because there wasn't much money left in the bank.

He sighed. Even if he got better what good would it do him? Would he ever be able to climb on a horse again? Ride across the land he loved so much? How could he check his herd?

He closed his eyes and thought back to the financial mess he'd left before he had the stroke. He'd planned to try and fix it, but hadn't gotten the chance. Now it was too late.

With the Lazy S gone, he would have nothing....

"Dad?"

Hearing Ana's voice, he opened his eyes. She was smiling at him as if she really wanted to be here.

She was so pretty. He raised his hand to touch her, and

she gasped. "Oh, Dad. You can use your hand. That's wonderful." She hugged him. He closed his eyes against the
emotions, suddenly realizing how starved he'd been for
the contact.

After the way he'd treated her and her sisters, how could
she be so loving toward him? He didn't deserve it, but he
never wanted to give it up. Yet, he knew he would have to.
Ana would be around only until he got better.

CHAPTER EIGHT

THREE DAYS LATER, Ana sat at her father's desk going over the ranch's finances. Things still weren't in great shape, with the extra payroll going to the men on the roundup, but thanks to the neighbors volunteering to help out, it could have been worse. Of course, the Lazy S would be returning the favor when those ranches needed help.

Vance had also worked out a deal with Garrett to transport the yearlings to the feedlot. In exchange, Vance was going to plant the Temple Ranch alfalfa crop next year.

She frowned, thinking about the first day of the roundup, and how patient the man had been with her. All these years her father had never wanted to make the effort, but Vance had taken the time to teach her about the operation.

She leaned back, thinking about the handsome cowboy with those deep-set eyes, the cocky smile and a mouth that tempted her. She never knew if he was serious about her or if she was just a challenge, the boss's daughter he'd always been forbidden to go near.

She liked to think that those shared kisses meant something to him, too. Yet since the roundup he'd been distant, staying far away from her, including the house. Okay, he'd been busy. Did that mean he had to spend all his time at the bunkhouse? Then today he'd moved back into the foreman's house.

She'd known it would happen sooner or later. What she didn't expect was to miss him so much. It was more than missing him; she'd come to care about Vance. More than she wanted to admit. If she let herself, she could fall in love with him. She suspected it was already too late.

The phone rang, bringing Ana out of her daydream. "Lazy S Ranch," she answered.

"You sound so official," a familiar voice said.

"Josie?"

"Yes, it's me," her sister said. "You're the only one who ever knew my voice from Tori's. How are things in Montana?"

"Looking better every day, " Ana fibbed a little.

There was a long pause, then Josie asked, "How is Colt doing?"

Ana had kept in touch with her sisters about everything going on. "I went to the rehab center yesterday. He's doing well. The therapist says he's improving every day. It won't be long before he comes home."

"That's good," Josie said, then asked, "How did the roundup go?"

Ana smiled. So her sister had been reading all the emails she'd sent. "The yearlings were shipped off to the feedlot." She didn't mention Garrett Temple's help, knowing the twosome's history. Not if she ever wanted Josie to return home.

Ana rushed on to say, "And we're booked solid for fishing through the fall. Even the foreman's house is rented the next two months."

Josie finally rejoined the conversation, "That's good, Ana, but as you say, we still need more income. Have you thought about expanding?"

"Expand how?" Ana asked, happy that one of her sisters, at least, cared.

"I've done several corporate events in the past few years. The most requested is to set up something in a different locale, where it's quiet and restful, a sort of retreat. If you are serious about having another income for the ranch, there needs to be more housing for larger gatherings. Then the ranch could be rented out for corporate functions, for special fishing events, or even for small weddings.

"That sounds like an expensive undertaking," Ana said, knowing they didn't have the money for such a big venture. "How are we going to finance a project of that scale?"

"Tori and I are working on that," Josie admitted.

Ana loved that the twins wanted to help, but how long it would take, and how much money, was a big worry. "Do you know someone with deep pockets?" she asked, half teasing.

"You might be surprised. Adding a silent partner could be an option."

"Not sure about that," Ana told her, then looked up and saw Vance standing in the doorway.

He leaned against the doorjamb, just watching her. She tried to focus on what her sister had to say, but the man's presence was distracting her. When his dark gaze locked on hers, her heart began to race so fast she had trouble concentrating. "Why don't you email me the information?"

Vance stood across the room. He knew he had acted like a jealous jerk, but he couldn't stay away from Ana any longer. And since he'd talked with Garrett, he knew there had been nothing between the two. His friend admitted he'd cared about Josie.

So Vance needed to apologize. He also knew it was time to find out how Ana felt about him. From the second she'd returned to the ranch, all those long-ago feelings had been stirred up again. He had to know if he was wasting time. If Ana didn't care about him at all, he needed to move on.

When she looked at him with her sapphire eyes, he couldn't seem to think about much of anything, except how much he wanted her. Before he lost his nerve, he walked into the office and closed the door behind him, his gaze never leaving Ana's.

She continued to talk to Josie, but if he had anything to do with it, the conversation was about to be cut off. He went around the desk and Ana's eyes grew large, but he didn't stop. He placed his hat in the overstuffed chair beside her, then took the phone from her hand.

He sat on the edge of the desk directly in front of her as he spoke into the receiver. "Hello, Josie. This is Vance. I have something important to talk to Ana about, so you'll have to call her back. Later." He hung up the phone.

Ana looked shocked. "Why did you do that?"

He pulled her to her feet, settled her between his legs as his arms went around her waist, bringing her even closer. "So I can do this."

He dipped his head and captured her lips. She remained stiff for a second or two, then slowly sighed as she melted into him. Soon she raised her hands around his neck and threaded her fingers through his hair.

Good Lord. No woman had ever felt as good as Ana. His tongue slipped inside and tasted her essence, only making him want her more. He finally tore his mouth away and looked at her.

Her eyes were wide with desire. "I take it you don't hate me anymore."

"I never did." He leaned his forehead against hers. "Just jealousy rearing its ugly head. I'm sorry."

"Why would you be jeal—"

He cut off the words when he kissed her again, and again. "Because I want you, Ana. I care about you."

Her eyes rounded. "Oh, Vance..." She drew a shaky

breath. "I'm not sure. If things don't work out between us…"

"How will we know if we don't give it a try?"

Her gaze searched his face. "What about Colt?"

"He's not here."

"He will be," she stated.

"Suddenly you need your daddy's approval?"

"It's not that, it's everything else. Along with Dad, we have a ranch to run together."

Vance was hurt that she had so many excuses, but he hid it with anger. He held her back so he could stand. "I guess that tells me what I needed to know." He reached for his hat, and was heading for the door when she called to him.

"Vance, it's not that…. I mean, if it doesn't work out…"

He gripped the brim of his hat. "Ana, why don't you think about it, and give me a call when you decide what you want?" He turned and walked out. A man had to have some pride, even when it came to love.

Sometime in the early morning, Ana got tired of rolling around in bed, and finally got up and went downstairs. She glanced at the clock; it wasn't even 4:00 a.m. Great. She poured herself a glass of juice and went to the large picture window behind the kitchen table.

She kept playing over and over in her head what Vance had said to her. *I want you.* She wanted him, too, but she was scared, scared to give her heart to a man. No, it was just this man. Vance had the power to hurt her, because she already cared about him.

She heard a noise behind her, then Kathleen appeared. "Sorry, did I wake you?"

"I was getting up anyway." Still in her pajamas and robe, the older woman came up to her, looking concerned. "Are you okay, Ana?"

"Yeah, I'm just a little restless."

The housekeeper had been a mother and a friend. "I suspect it's more than that."

Ana started to deny it, but Kathleen interrupted. "Could you be missing a certain man since he moved out of the house?"

"Crazy, isn't it? Most of the time we can't even be civil to each other." Ana couldn't stop thinking about what had happened in the office earlier.

Kathleen sighed. "Sweetheart, you two have been dancing around each other since you came back here to live." In the predawn quiet, Ana could hear Kathleen's humor. "So have you decided to do anything about it?"

Was that it? Did she feel safer dancing around the issue without risking her heart? "Me? Why should I do something?"

She was met with silence.

"Maybe I'm scared," Ana admitted.

"Love is scary. Don't let what happened to your parents stop you." Kathleen turned to her. "All I can tell you is what I know. Vance Rivers is a good man. But when it comes to love there are always chances things won't work. You have to decide if you're willing to take it."

Ana never was one to take risks. She was the oldest, the sensible daughter. She always tried to do the right thing. So why was she walking across the compound to Vance's house just before dawn?

She was afraid to answer that question. She was shaking as she walked up the steps, but before she could chicken out, she knocked on the door. She stood there a few minutes and almost felt relieved when there wasn't an answer. Just as she started to leave, the door opened and Vance stood there, wearing only a pair of jeans and a towel draped around his neck.

Oh, God. She loved looking at this man. She met his eyes and tried desperately to speak, but nothing came out of her mouth.

"What the hell." He reached for her, pulled her into the house and closed the door, pushing her back against it. A soft light came from over the stove in the kitchen, letting her see the look of desire in his eyes.

"What are you doing here?"

"I didn't like how we left things last night."

"So you thought coming here before dawn was a wise thing to do?"

"I couldn't sleep."

"Join the club, lady. You've kept invading my dreams since you've come home."

His honesty shocked her. "Really?"

In answer, he lowered his head and covered her mouth with his. With a soft moan, she gripped his bare arms, feeling his strength. Yet he held her with tenderness as he placed teasing kisses against her lips.

"We could bring my dreams to life if you like," he told her before he gave her another sample. He captured her mouth in a deep kiss, causing her knees to give out.

He wrapped his arms around her, pulling her close. "I got you," he whispered.

She laid her head against his chest, feeling his rapid heartbeat. "I want you, Vance," she breathed.

He pulled back and looked down at her. A slow smile crossed his face. "That's nice to know, but your timing is rotten. I promised Garrett I'd help him out this morning."

"Oh…" What should she do now? She pulled away. "Okay. Sure. I should leave and let you get going."

"Wait." Vance tugged her back into his arms. His gaze

moved over her face as his hand cupped her cheek. "I'm just as disappointed as you are. When I make love to you, Ana, I don't want to rush it. I want to take hours," he breathed as his lips brushed over her ear. "I want to spend all night making slow sweet love to you." He raised his head and covered her mouth again. He was breathing hard when he drew back. "I don't want to leave you right now."

She shivered, her own breathing rapid and her imagination running wild. "I don't want to go, either," she admitted. Suddenly she didn't have any pride when it came to this man.

"Tonight. Come to dinner with me, tonight?"

"A date?"

His smile faded. "Is there a problem with going out with me?"

"No. It's just…that I promised Colt I'd drop by tonight."

"I should be back from Garrett's by three. I can go with you, then we could have dinner."

She suddenly brightened. "I'd like that."

"Okay, it's a *date*," he said, leaving no doubt that he wanted to spend time with her.

"A date." She started for the door, but he quickly pulled her back and covered her mouth again. By the time the kiss ended she was light-headed. "I'll see you later."

She managed to walk out the door, but she wasn't sure if her feet ever touched the ground as she made her way back to the house.

Ana hadn't been out on a date in so long she was having trouble deciding what to wear. She settled for white linen trousers and a sleeveless, peach-colored blouse and heeled sandals.

When she came down the steps, Vance was waiting for her. He was dressed in black Wrangler jeans, a slate-gray

Western shirt and shiny boots, and had his black Stetson in his hand.

His smile sent a warm shiver up her spine. "You look beautiful." He stepped forward and took her into his arms. His head dipped, and he placed a tender kiss against her lips.

"Thank you," she said. "You don't look so bad yourself." She was reaching for her purse when Kathleen walked out.

"You two have a good time," she called.

"We will," Vance said as he escorted her to his clean truck. The inside was spotless, too. "Someone's been busy today," she said as he climbed into the driver's side.

He leaned across the console. "I have this special girl I was hoping to impress." His mouth brushed over hers again, and she sucked in a breath. He pulled away before it got too intense. "Have I succeeded?"

"I'll let you know later."

Thirty minutes later, Vance escorted Ana into the rehab center. He found he was nervous. What would Colt think about him going out with his daughter? Even though Ana was an adult, Vance still couldn't help but wonder if Colt would think he was good enough.

He shook off the feeling. Neither he nor Ana were planning to make an announcement to the man. There wasn't anything to say, anyway. Not yet.

At Colt's room they found the door partly opened and the speech therapist inside. Vance froze when he heard the sounds coming from Colt.

"Dad," Ana cried as she went into the room. "You're talking."

Colt's therapist, Carrie Woodridge, stood up. "Ms. Slater, I wasn't expecting you."

Vance noted the panicked look on Colt's face. He wasn't

ready to share his accomplishments. "Ana, why don't we leave until Carrie is finished?" He took her by the hand. "We'll come back."

He looked at the therapist and she signaled about thirty minutes. With a tug on Ana's hand, he managed to get her out the door.

"But, Vance… I want to help."

"But your father doesn't want you to hear him stumble over his words. You know how proud Colt is."

Smiling, Ana nodded. "He's talking, Vance. I can't believe how much progress he's made since coming here." She glanced around the state-of-the-art facility. "I'm just worried about the cost."

"Isn't the insurance company covering it all?"

She sighed. "Finding that out wasn't on the top of my list when Dad needed a place for rehab."

Vance had some concerns, too, but he didn't want Ana worrying. He glanced at his watch. "Let's go and check with the billing department. It's early yet. And if we discover there's money owed, we'll figure out something. Colt needs to be here."

They walked back to the reception area and asked to speak to someone in the accounting department. Moments later, a young, dark-haired woman came through the double doors. She saw them and smiled. "Ms. Slater. I'm Allison Garcia. I understand you need to discuss your father's coverage."

"Yes. We're not sure what the insurance covers on his bill."

The woman nodded, then escorted them back to her office and had them sit down in front of her desk.

"First of all, are you happy with your father's care here at Morningside Rehab Facility?"

"Very much so," Ana said. "He's been improving at a remarkable pace."

Allison smiled again. "Good."

Ana exchanged a look with Vance. "We're just wondering about the cost."

The accountant turned to her computer and brought up the file. "Your father's insurance is handling eighty percent."

"So twenty percent is our responsibility?"

Allison looked over the paper. "It appears there's been an adjustment in the bill." She glanced at Ana. "A lot of times, they adjust the cost for patients."

"So there isn't a balance owing?"

"As of right now, there isn't." Allison smiled. "We're a new facility, and we're trying to build a reputation in this area. I'd say your father is a recipient of this good fortune, so the cost has been adjusted."

"That's wonderful," Ana said as she stood, then thanked the woman for her time and left.

"Do you feel better now?" Vance asked as they walked out into the reception area.

"I don't know. It's nice that Dad has the cushion of a discount, but I'm afraid of all the other bills that are coming in. We're trying to keep the ranch afloat and we're barely making it."

Vance took her by the hand and directed her into a deserted passageway. "You've got to stop this, Ana. You can't do it all alone." He leaned down and brushed his mouth over hers. "I'm here, too. We'll figure this out together. Somehow we'll come up with other ideas about making money."

She nodded. "Thank you."

"Stop thanking me. We're in this together. I don't want to lose the Lazy S, either. It's been my home for nearly eighteen years." He touched her cheek. "That's how long I've cared about you."

* * *

Colt was exhausted from his speech session, and from having Ana walk in. He hadn't been ready for anyone to know that he could speak, especially Ana. Not yet.

He could still see the look on Vance's face. He would be harder to fool about his progress. Colt never could put much past that boy. Of course, Vance River was a good man, and Colt also saw the way he looked at Ana. There was no hiding his desire for her. And there was no doubt there was something going on between them.

Colt grabbed his walker and worked to stand up, then managed to get himself over to the window to look out at the mountains he loved.

He thought back over his life, to the happiness of those first few years with Luisa and their daughters, until everything had fallen apart.

Vance had come into his life by accident. Having him show up at the ranch had distracted Colt from a lot of his pain. He'd had to concentrate on the kid, who'd been so wild he barely had table manners. Vance had also been suspicious toward anyone in authority. Colt couldn't blame him. Everyone who'd said they loved him had just abused him.

The one thing Colt had had to do was keep Vance away from his daughters.

He glanced down into the parking lot now and caught a glimpse of the couple walking toward the truck. Vance tugged on Ana's hand and pulled her into his arms and kissed her.

Colt couldn't stop them. He smiled. Of course, why would he want to?

CHAPTER NINE

AT SEVEN O'CLOCK, Vance escorted Ana into a small restaurant just outside Dillon that was nestled up to the river's bank. The Riverside Inn was well known for its seafood and prime rib.

The hostess led them across the small, intimate dining room to a booth with a view of the river. Ana slid into her seat and Vance sat down across from her. She looked out at the picturesque scene, the late-day sun reflecting off the flowing water, creating a golden glow.

She smiled at her date. "It's lovely here."

"You've never been here?"

She shook her head. "I really don't go out much."

"So Sawhill never brought you here?"

She was taken aback by the question, but quickly shook her head. "As I said before, we only went out a few times. We usually just went to Montana Mick's for drinks, and dancing."

Vance reached across the table and took her hand. "I apologize. I had no business asking you about your personal life, but you deserve better than a guy who thinks that a few drinks is a way to treat a lady."

She knew that, but Mike had been the only man asking to spend time with her. "It was just a casual thing."

"Well, I want to make some special memories with you,

Ana. And if you want to go dancing, I'll take you to Montana's, or anywhere else."

Suddenly, she found it difficult to breathe. "I like being right here…with you."

He gave her a big smile. "I can do that, bright eyes."

Another catch in her breath. "Why do you call me that?"

He shrugged. "Because your eyes are the prettiest blue…and so expressive. They were the first thing I ever noticed about you."

She blinked at his admission. "You mean when you came to live at the ranch?"

He nodded.

"You were barely fourteen. I was twelve."

He winked. "That's old enough to be attracted to a pretty girl." He squeezed her hand again. "And now she's turned into a beautiful woman."

Ana found her heart pounding, not over the compliment, but that she was feeling the same attraction. And less than twenty-four hours ago she'd gone to Vance's house in hopes of ending up in his bed.

Oh, God. What had gotten into her? She'd never approached men. Maybe that was why she'd spent so many years alone. Wasn't it about time she went after what she wanted?

"You're going to wear yourself out, thinking so hard."

She felt the heat rising to her neck. "It's Colt," she said, wanting to change the subject. Facing her feelings for Vance wasn't something she was ready to deal with. "Did he seem okay to you when we went back to his room?"

Vance wasn't sure if he should say anything, because he didn't want to change her good mood. "Your father is fine, outside of the fact that he knows I have a thing for his daughter. I'm not sure he likes the idea." Vance raised her hand to his mouth and placed a kiss against her knuckles. "He saw how I looked at you today."

Ana's mouth dropped open. "Why would he care?"

"I think that Colt has always cared about you girls. He was just afraid to show it."

"Afraid? We loved our dad. We showered him with affection until he pushed us away so many times we couldn't handle any more rejection."

Vance felt Ana's sadness. He leaned closer and lowered his voice. "I only knew about Luisa from Kathleen."

Ana tensed at her mother's name, and he gripped her hand tighter. "It's hard to figure why she left her husband and four daughters, but there was no doubt that Colt loved her." Vance stared into Ana's eyes. "Someone you care about deeply isn't so easy to get over." His gaze locked on hers. "I know."

He watched her throat work. "There's been a special woman in your life?" she murmured.

He wanted to lay his heart out then and there and tell her of his feelings, but all he could manage was a nod before the waitress appeared at their table. Vance ordered prime rib rare and Ana asked for the same.

"Will there be anything else? A drink from the bar?"

He turned to Ana. "Would you like a glass of wine?"

"Only if you are, too," she said.

He shook his head. "I'm having iced tea."

"I'll have the same."

After the waitress left, Ana asked, "Is the reason you don't like to drink because of your dad?"

Vance released a breath, trying to stay relaxed. His past was something he never liked talking about. "I haven't considered Calvin Rivers my father for a long time. But yes, he's the reason I don't drink in public. I don't want to give people the chance to think I'm anything like him."

Ana nodded. "Do you keep in touch?"

He shook his head. "Are you kidding? He lit out of town right after Colt took me in." The last thing Vance wanted was to bring up the past to darken the mood. "Why don't we make a pact tonight and not talk about any family?"

She smiled and agreed.

"What about you, Ana? You like your job?" He already knew a lot about her life. He'd made it his business to know about the woman he'd never managed to forget. The woman he couldn't get over.

She smiled again. "There isn't much to tell. You already know I'm a counselor at the high school. I love my job. At first I thought I wanted to teach, but I enjoy helping the students with their long-term goals. So many people want kids to pick a career, but never take the time to guide them and show them all their options."

He loved hearing her enthusiasm. He'd seen firsthand the respect and admiration Ana generated when he'd talked with two of her students, Billy and Justin, at the roundup.

"And I would say you're good at your job."

She shrugged. "I hope I am, because the kids mean a lot to me."

Vance leaned forward, wishing he could get closer to her. "You coming tonight means a lot to me, too, Ana. I hope I can convince you just how much."

He watched her eyes grow wide, but before she could say anything, their food arrived. He'd put his feelings out there; now it was her move.

Over the next two days, Ana couldn't stop thinking about her evening with Vance. It had been incredible. When they'd driven back to the ranch, however, he'd walked her up the steps to the house, gave her a toe-curling kiss, then said good-night and left. She hadn't seen him since.

With a sigh, she sat down at the desk in the office. On paper the Lazy S was showing some profit. The bills were getting paid, and a lot of the back payments for the lease were being made up. As for the day-to-day operations, they still needed a steadier income. There was nothing in reserve.

Ana printed out the email her sister Josie had sent her yesterday. It was a list of different websites Ana could go to and see advisements from other ranches that had gone into side businesses. Some had added the dude ranch element; another showed a large, all-purpose structure they rented out for corporate retreats, small weddings, even quilting workshops. All these places were also working cattle operations.

Ana had to admit there were some good ideas. Problem was, they would need capital to build the extra structures. She doubted that any bank would loan them money with the ranch barely making it.

There was a knock on the door and Vance stuck his head in. He'd been out working, because he still had those sexy leather chaps on over his dusty jeans.

She felt the heat move through her body as he smiled, removed his hat and asked, "You busy?"

"Nothing that can't wait," she managed to answer.

He walked in and came around the desk and tugged on her hand so she would stand. "First, I need to do this." He lowered his head and his mouth captured hers. The kiss started out sweet, gentle. It quickly changed when he took charge and pulled her closer as their need intensified. By the time he released her they were both breathless.

"I've missed you," he said.

"I've been here, but I didn't know where you were." Okay, so she was a little hurt that he couldn't make time for her. Or maybe he'd decided that he didn't want to carry things between them any further.

"I've been at Bill Perkins's place. He broke his arm last week so I've been helping with the roundup. I was going to tell you yesterday, but you'd already left to go see Colt. I told Kathleen."

"Oh, I haven't seen her today." Ana knew she was being foolish, because Vance hadn't made any promises to her.

He smiled and she got all warm and achy inside.

"So you missed me?" he drawled.

She smacked his arm and pulled back. "Don't get a big head about it. Besides, we have a ranch to run, so it's nice to know where you are."

Vance wasn't happy to have to report in to her, as if he couldn't do his job. "The men were taking care of things, but you're right, I should have called you directly to let you know." He kissed the end of her nose. "I tried to finish up at a good time yesterday, but it didn't work out that way. As badly as I wanted to talk to you, it was too late to phone." He pulled her close and nuzzled her neck, sending shivers up her spine. "Do I get points for not being able to think about anything but you?"

Oh, yes. "Maybe."

"Were you thinking about me?"

"I've been too busy." His lips were touching all the right spots. "Oh, Vance," she gasped.

He raised his head and gave her a cocky smile. "Seems I hit a sensitive spot. How many more do you have?"

She was in big trouble. She managed to step away. "I need to get back to work."

Vance let her go, but he wasn't about to leave yet. He pulled up a chair and sat down beside her at the desk. He liked inhaling her scent, and would like to keep tasting her, but she'd probably throw him out if he pushed too hard.

"So I hear we have more guests arriving this weekend. That has to be good."

She nodded. "The business we've gotten from the anglers is good. But we still need to expand to make enough to keep the ranch going." She showed him some of the websites of ranches branching out with things other than just raising cattle.

He liked the ideas, but what would Colt think about it? "Have you talked with Hank Clarkson about this, to see if it would be worth the expense of expanding?" Vance asked. "Would we be able to fill more rooms than just the foreman's house?"

Ana looked at him. They were so close he could lean in and kiss that sweet mouth of hers. He watched her eyes darken. It was nice to know that she was feeling the same heat.

She turned back to the computer. "There are other groups we can cater to than just anglers. Josie suggests we think on a larger scale. If we build a main structure, we should think about doing corporate retreats. We could handle small weddings, quilting retreats. Surprisingly, there are all sorts of groups that enjoy time in the country."

Vance looked back at the screen. "It sounds like there are a lot of options."

She nodded. "Problem is we don't have a lot of money for construction." She sighed as she pointed to the log cabin–style building in the picture. "This would be perfect by the group of trees beside the river. I've even come up with a name, the River's Edge."

Vance liked these suggestions. "We could talk to a contractor and get an estimate on costs, then present it to the bank."

Ana's eyes lit up. "So you think it's worth it?"

"Yeah, I do. We can't get crazy, but maybe we could

start off with a central structure." Vance pointed to the log
house on the screen. He, too, was caught up in the idea.
"The downstairs could have a main meeting room, plus
a kitchen, and the upstairs, three or four bedrooms. That
would bring in some money. Then later we could add some
cabins along the river, for the anglers, or for corporate
functions. Between the foreman's house and a few cabins,
we could double our income."

She rewarded him with a smile that made his gut tighten
in need. He wanted to take her into his arms and make her
forget about everything else but them. Soon. They had a
lot to deal with right now. But one day, it was going to be
all about them. He wasn't going to let her leave the ranch
again. Not without a fight.

The next evening, Ana watched Vance walk toward the
house carrying his duffel bag. Once again he'd moved out
of the foreman's house for a group of anglers coming in
for the weekend. This time, instead of going to the bunkhouse, he was back at the main house. A welcome sight
for her, but also frightening, since closeness could mean
their relationship could move to the next level.

Was she ready for that? She recalled her early morning walk to his house a week ago, when she'd been more
than willing to move ahead with a relationship. It had been
Vance who'd slowed things down. He'd gone with her to
visit to her father, taken her on the roundup. And there was
their date the other night. She shivered, recalling when he'd
showed up in the office and kissed the daylights out of her.
He seemed to care about her.

She was definitely falling hard for this man. What
frightened her was she didn't want to be just one of Vance
River's women. A few years back, the man had been

seen with several different women, but none of them ever seemed to last long.

What did he want with her?

All Ana knew was that she had come to care about him, a lot. She could admit it now. She'd cared about him years ago, but also resented him for taking her father's attention. She couldn't blame him any longer. That was all Colt's doing.

So what should she do now?

She heard a sound and turned around as Vance walked into the kitchen.

He smiled and winked, then walked up to Kathleen. "Smells good. Is supper about ready?"

She nudged him out of her way. "Sit down and I'll bring you a plate."

Ana had the table set and ready, but was she ready for this man? She couldn't ignore the feelings she had whenever Vance was close to her.

"How was your afternoon?" he asked.

"I stayed busy."

He placed the napkin on his lap. "Did you get in to see Colt?"

She nodded as Kathleen brought over the pot roast and potatoes. "It was a short visit, but he was sitting in the recreation room."

Vance paused. "No kidding. Was Colt making friends?"

She shook her head. "He was watching television."

They continued to share their day, and Ana enjoyed the relaxed time with him and Kathleen. But every so often, she'd catch Vance watching her. She couldn't stop the blush and he'd smile.

"Kathleen, the meal was great. Thanks." He looked at Ana. "I'm going to the barn to check on the horses before turning in."

She nodded and helped Kathleen finish loading the dishwasher.

"My, my, seems a little warm in here tonight. Are you two any closer to admitting your feelings?" the housekeeper asked when they were alone.

Ana looked at her. "Vance has been keeping his distance since our date. So I'm not sure what he wants."

"You might try pushing the issue."

Ana wasn't sure if she could pull off a seduction, but she wanted Vance.

After taking her shower, she put on a gown and the bathrobe Kathleen had given her for her birthday. The lightweight, rose-colored silk felt cool against her skin. She was brushing her hair when she heard someone coming up the stairs. Vance.

Her heart raced at the sound of him entering the bedroom down the hall. She sighed in relief, until once again there were footsteps, coming in her direction, and ending at the bathroom across from her room. Soon the water came on in the shower.

Ten minutes later, Ana took a breath and released it as she opened her bedroom door and waited. Somehow, she had to let Vance Rivers know she was ready to have a real relationship.

Vance quickly dried off and realized he hadn't brought any clean clothes with him. He'd been so distracted by Ana he wasn't sure what he was doing, or what he wanted to do. Although it was killing him, he couldn't rush her and mess this up. Maybe moving back to this house wasn't a good idea.

He wrapped the towel around his waist and gathered his dirty jeans, then opened the door, to be met by Ana standing in her doorway.

"Hey. Sorry, I didn't mean to hold you up from using the bathroom."

"You didn't." She came toward him. "I was waiting for you."

Oh, boy. His gaze moved over her short, silky robe and bare legs, and his body stirred to life. So much for the cold shower.

Giving up any idea of backing off, he walked up to her. "I've been waiting for you forever, Ana. So be sure this is what you want, because I'm not going to give you up."

Ana worked to swallow the dryness in her throat. This step could be disastrous, but she also knew it could be wonderful, and she was willing to take a chance on this man she'd fallen in love with. Maybe she'd even loved him for years.

She nodded. "I want to be with you, too, Vance."

He took her hand and walked her to his bedroom, then pulled her inside and closed the door. He tossed his dirty clothes aside and leaned down and captured her mouth. She went willingly and kissed him back with the same fervor. She was quickly consumed by desire for this man as his tongue slipped past her parted lips, making her body crave even closer contact.

He finally released her, but his mouth moved to her ear and he whispered, "I want you, too, bright eyes. And I plan to prove just how much when I kiss every delicate inch of you." His lips moved over her jaw, placing tiny kisses as he went. Next he trailed a path down her neck, causing her to shiver. When her knees started to give out, he caught her. "I got you, Ana."

Her lips parted as she worked to breathe against the rush of feelings he created inside her. Her hands went to his chest, moving and stroking over the hard planes of his bare skin.

He was busy, too, working on the knot of the belt on her robe. When it parted, he pushed the garment off her shoulders, then stood back to gaze at her. Finally, he reached up and tugged on the straps of her nightgown, pulling it down her arms to drop at her waist.

"God, Ana, you're beautiful."

He tugged her into his arms and kissed her deeply. Then he swung her up, carried her across the room, set her down beside the bed and took off her remaining clothes. Once she was naked, he stood back and eyed her closely.

She reached for his towel and let it drop, then touched his bare chest. "You are beautiful, too." She felt shaky as she placed kisses along his skin. He sucked in a strained breath as he cupped her face, then his mouth covered hers again.

He finally pulled back. "Are you sure about this, Ana?" His gaze was dark and riveting. "This isn't a game to me. Once we're together, I don't plan to let you go."

She took that leap of faith, trusted her feelings for this man. "Yes, I'm sure. I want you, Vance, only you."

Sometime around dawn the next morning, Ana rolled over in bed and blinked as she saw Vance pulling on his jeans. She smiled, then realized he was leaving.

"Vance?" she whispered in the darkness.

He turned and she took in his broad shoulders and chest. Once again her heart set off racing.

"Hey, I didn't mean to wake you. I need to go get the men started for the day." He sat down on the bed. "I'm already running late as it is."

She sat up and slipped her arms around his neck, causing the sheet to drop to her waist. "Then it shouldn't hurt if you stay with me a little longer."

"What about Kathleen?"

"Let her find her own man."

Ana placed her mouth against his and did her best to distract him. With a groan, he surrendered, wrapping his arms around her and deepening the kiss. By the time he broke it off, they were both breathless.

"Lady, you don't play fair." He stood. "I really need to go. Not just for me, but for you, too. I know the men aren't going to think anything about me walking out of this house, but I would like to keep this between us for the time being. I want this special for us."

Suddenly, Vance had some doubts. "Unless you don't want any more than last night."

She looked at him for what seemed like an eternity, then rose up and punched him in the arm. "You didn't say that, did you?"

"Hey." He rubbed his biceps, but was happy she was offended by his remark. "I'm just giving you options."

"If you don't know me better than that, then we're done here."

He reached for her and pulled her back into his arms. Closing his eyes, he reveled in the feeling of her pressed again him. "Hey, cut me some slack. Last night was special to me. More than you'll ever know. I don't want you to have any regrets."

She raised her head. "For me, too, Vance." She touched his face. "I want to be with you, and not just here." Then those beautiful baby blues looked at him. "I care about you."

"I care about you, too." He leaned down and kissed her. He was a goner when it came to this woman. As the kiss deepened, he pressed her back against the mattress, needing to feel closer to her. He couldn't leave Ana now, maybe never. Just this once, he'd let the men handle the work, and he'd take the morning off.

CHAPTER TEN

"YOU KNOW YOU can't keep fooling everyone much longer."

Colt sat in his wheelchair and stared at his therapist, trying to act clueless about the accusations. But Jay knew him too well. The young man hadn't been intimidated, and matched Colt's stubbornness throughout the past month.

"Your daughter is going to discover your secret before long."

Colt wanted to tell him to stay out of his life, but knew what he said was true. He shook his head. "N...no."

Ana had been coming to see him nearly every day. Would she keep visiting him if she knew that he was improving so quickly?

"N-not r-ready yet."

The young man placed his hands on his hips. "Do you realize, Colt Slater, how lucky you are to be recovering at this rate? Whatever your reason for playing helpless, it's going to backfire. Ana's been so worried about you."

"Sh...she said that?" Colt raised his arm. It was still weak, but he could move it now.

The last thing he wanted was to lose Ana again. She'd moved back home to help out. Every visit, she talked in detail about what was going on. It had been a highlight of his day—not hearing about the ranch, but hearing it from her. He knew it was a long shot, but he hoped he could start to rebuild their relationship. He just didn't know where to begin.

All those years he'd wasted on bitterness toward the girls' mother, he'd lost any connection to his daughters. He didn't want to go back to that big, empty house. "Sh-she won't c-come to see me any...anymore."

Before Jay answered, a knock at the door distracted them. Vance peered inside. "I don't mean to disturb you. I can come back later."

"No, we're finished for the day," Jay said, then looked back at his patient. "Think about what I said, Colt."

Vance walked into the room. Alone. "Ana couldn't make it today. She had to go to a meeting at the school."

Vance didn't miss the disappointment on Colt's face. So he *did* want Ana to visit. Maybe the stroke would change some things between father and daughter. Maybe he would finally realize what he had.

"Sorry, you get me instead."

Colt made a groaning sound and turned away. Vance wondered if the man's attitude had something to with him having a relationship with his daughter.

Jay checked his watch. "I need to go to my next session. I'll be by tomorrow, Colt. So behave until then."

Vance said goodbye, then grabbed a chair and placed it in front of Colt's wheelchair. He straddled it and rested his forearms on the back.

"So what's new?"

Colt frowned. "Y...you t-tell me."

Vance was thrilled that Colt was talking. "You know most of it from Ana. The yearlings were branded, shipped and sold last week. The foreman's house has been rented out to three anglers for the weekend, and Hank Clarkson is taking them fly-fishing to that sweet spot at the river where your daughters used to swim."

"Wh…where?"

"Don't play dumb, Colt. We both know you used to go check on the girls."

Again he frowned.

Vance ignored it. "We're showing a decent profit from the fishing, so we can probably pay off the leases. It's not enough, though. Your daughter Josie is talking about branching out."

Vance went on to explain about some of the changes they'd been talking about, the ideas about building a new structure.

He saw the angry look on Colt's face before the older man glanced away.

"Don't be upset. We're doing this to help save the Lazy S."

Colt looked back and nodded. "T-take c-care of Ana."

Vance was surprised by his words. "I will, always. I care about her. She will be pleased to know you're able to talk."

Colt raised his hand. "No! D-don't tell her. Keep my s…secret."

Vance stared at him a moment, then said, "I will, but I think you're making a mistake."

Colt wanted a chance to repair some damage, praying it wasn't too late. He needed Ana there at the ranch when he returned home. "N…not the first one."

Later that day in the barn, Ana could sense Vance even before he touched her. His hands slipped around her waist, and she stopped brushing Blondie's coat, then leaned back as he pulled her against his hard body. "I missed you," he whispered against her ear as he placed kisses along her neck.

"You saw me this morning," she told him, recalling how he had climbed out of bed after making love.

"Five o'clock was a long time ago. Do you have any idea how hard it was to leave you?"

"Oh, Vance." She shivered as his mouth caused goose bumps along her skin. Unable to stand much more, she turned in his arms and quickly brushed her lips across his.

Vance released a groan as he captured her mouth in a deep, searing kiss. He finally released her. "If you're going to greet me like that, I should go away more often."

Ana didn't want him to leave her ever, but she knew that in a few more weeks she had to go back to her job and her life in town. She had no clue as to what would happen with their relationship. Was it even a relationship? There hadn't been any declaration or promises.

"No, this ranch couldn't run without you."

He cupped her face. "You're doing a good job, too. The men seem eager to do whatever you want."

Good, maybe he was a little jealous. "Does that bother you?"

He placed a quick kiss on her lips. "Not if they're doing their jobs. And if they aren't trying to steal my girl."

His girl. Ana froze, trying to draw air into her lungs. Suddenly the horse shifted and nudged them against the stall railing.

He chuckled. "I think we're crowding Blondie. I know of a better place," he suggested. "It's about a twenty-minute horseback ride. You game?"

Blondie whinnied and Ana smiled.

"I take it that's a yes."

Thirty minutes later Ana was on Blondie and racing toward the meadow. She glanced over her shoulder, seeing Vance atop Rusty, closing on her.

"Come on, girl. We can't let them beat us." Ana leaned forward and nudged the mare with her heels. Feeling the wind on her face and being in rhythm with her horse gave her a feeling of peace. She caught sight of Vance coming up beside her, but she stayed the course and didn't let the gorgeous man distract her.

She smiled. He'd already distracted her. She'd fallen so hard, she couldn't think about anything else. When the small cabin came into view, she pulled back on the reins. Blondie slowed and finally stopped next to the sagging porch.

Vance rode in, climbed down, and after tying his horse to the rail, walked toward her. "You are one sexy lady, but when you're on horseback, you are incredible." He bent down and kissed her.

She loved that she could make him feel this way. "Don't try and distract me with your compliments."

Vance refused to let her go. "So I can distract you. That's good to know." His mouth came down on hers once more. This time he took her lips in a hungry kiss, knowing how quickly this woman could go to his head, not to mention his heart. He'd lost that to her at about age fourteen. He drew her to him, and she sank her sweet body against him. He ached for her. It also reminded him of the intimacy they'd shared last night and this morning. How much he wanted to have her that close always.

He broke off the kiss. His breathing was labored as he took a step back. "We'd better slow down or…" He stopped talking and walked toward the shack.

She followed him. "Vance?"

He turned around and could see the question in those beautiful blue eyes. "You keep looking at me like that, Ana, and I'm going to forget all my good intentions."

She smiled. "What are your intentions?"

"Look, last night was incredible."

She didn't seem happy. "But…?"

He went back to her. "There is no but, Ana." He gripped her by the shoulders. "I just don't want to mess up what's going on between us. I care about you."

"And I care about you, too."

He liked that, but was still worried. They had a lot of baggage between them. There were things she needed to know, about him and about this land. "There are a lot of things we have to deal with before it's just about us."

She nodded, then grabbed his hand and pulled him toward the shack, pushing open the stuck door. "Come with me to my special place."

They went inside the dusty, one-room cabin.

"I don't think we can use this place for the anglers," Vance joked.

She smacked his arm. "Nor would I want you to. This is mine. I know it's not much, not perfect, but it has this."

She went to the window over the rusted sink and pulled back the curtains, exposing an incredible view. Before them was the green, grassy meadow, encircled by glorious, tree-covered mountains that seemed to reach all the way to the big, blue Montana sky.

"It's perfect, Vance."

He heard the reverence in her voice as he came up behind her and wrapped his arms around her. "Yes, it is." He never doubted that Ana loved the Lazy S Ranch as much as he did. How would she feel if she knew that he was intruding on her heritage? He had his own plans for this meadow, and soon, he wanted to share them the woman in his arms.

Ana glanced over her shoulder and smiled at him. "I can imagine a hundred years ago, when my ancestors stood right here in this spot and gazed out at this same view. This cabin was built by my great-great-grandfather, Owen Colton. He and his bride, Millie, settled right here. Dad is named after that side of the family."

Vance envied Ana's connection to her roots. "So it wasn't Slaters who settled here."

"No, but not long after, my great-grandfather, George Slater, arrived on the scene."

"Did Colt tell you all this?"

She frowned. "Not hardly, but I looked it up in the town history. The Coltons and the Slaters practically build Royerton."

"What about your mother's side?"

He caught Ana's reaction. "I don't know anything about her."

"I think you do, just that you don't want to talk about her."

She glared. "Not any more than you want to talk about your parents."

He found he could trust her. "You can ask me anything you want."

She turned around and leaned against the sink. "Do you know where they are?"

"My father, no. My mother lived in southern Oklahoma with husband number three until she died about five years ago. Her drug-induced lifestyle finally caught up with her." He shrugged, purposely leaving out a lot of details. "Too many bad choices."

"I'm sorry, Vance."

"Like I said, she made bad choices." He released a breath. "Now, you. Where is your mother's family from?"

Ana wasn't sure she could talk about Luisa Delgado. Then she looked up into Vance's eyes and saw the compassion there. "Colt never spoke much about our mother's family. All I know is that she came from Ciudad Juarez, Mexico. At least that was the name of the town that was on the divorce papers."

"You saw the divorce papers?"

She shrugged. "It was a few months later. One night, I woke up, hearing some yelling downstairs. I came out of my room and saw the lady who used to take care of us, Mrs. Copeland, and Dad. She had her suitcase packed, and walked out the door. I hoped she was going away for good, since I didn't like her much.

"After a little while I went downstairs looking for Colt and found him lying on the sofa. He'd been drinking and was mumbling Luisa's name over and over again, saying she was never coming back. I stayed with him until he fell asleep." Ana brushed away a tear. "On the coffee table were some papers. There wasn't much I could recognize, except for the words *divorce decree* and the names Colton Slater and Luisa Delgado Slater."

His chest tightened, feeling her pain. "Have you ever thought about going to find her and ask her why she left you all?"

"Only every day during my childhood. I desperately wanted to find the woman who used to hug and kiss us every morning and every night. Who told us repeatedly that she loved us. Then one day she was gone." Ana felt tears welling in her eyes, but refused to let them fall. "But I couldn't will her to come back to her little girls. The worst thing was she took our father away, too. Colt never got over his sadness."

Vance pulled Ana into his arms. "I'm sorry, Ana. I wish I could do something." He leaned down and kissed her, wishing he could take away the pain for both of them. He wanted to erase all the hurt from the past and look toward the future. Would he have that future with Ana? Would there be more nights like last night when he got a glimmer of that dream? Yet there was so much that could keep that from happening for them.

"We should get back. It's getting late."

She looked disappointed. "But I don't want to leave. I like it here." She wrapped her arms around his waist. "It's magical."

"Magical?"

"As a girl, when I got the chance to go horseback riding, I came here. This meadow always made me feel better, so I named it the magic meadow." She smiled and shifted in his arms. "And now you're here."

Vance glanced around at the filthy room. "Not that you aren't tempting, Ana, but when the sun goes down, it won't seem so magical. Come on, I'll take you out to dinner, then we'll turn in early."

"Really?" Ana was excited that Vance was asking her out. "But I'm sure Kathleen has fixed us supper."

He shook his head. "It's her bingo night, so we're on our own for the evening. I thought we could go into town to the Big Sky Grill. I have some news about a contractor."

She gasped. "Tell me."

He shook his head. "We'll talk about it over supper. Right now, I want to take my girl out."

His girl? She tried not to turn all giddy on him. "Okay, it's a date. I'll race you back." She took off for her mount, suddenly loving her life at the ranch, and her man. The bad memories were turning into good ones.

An hour later, Vance walked Ana into the Big Sky Grill. Several heads turned in their direction. Okay, so they would be labeled a couple now. Good, he wanted everyone to know that Ana Slater was his.

They got the circular booth in the corner. He slid in on the other side from her and they met in the middle. She glanced over the menu, then closed it.

He stared. "So you know what you want?"

She nodded slowly and a sexy glint appeared in her eyes. "I have for a while."

Suddenly his heart began to race. "So have I. Ana…" He started to reach for her hand, but the waitress appeared and set down their water. After taking their order, she left.

Ana turned to him. "What were you about to say?"

Now wasn't the time to talk about their personal life. He glanced around at the crowd. "I'll tell you later. Let's talk business first."

She sighed and sat up straighter. "Yes, tell me about the contractor."

"Nothing is settled, but we talked a little about the building we want, and how our timeline is before winter, when the snow comes. His company is in Butte, but he's working from here now."

"Who?"

"Garrett Temple, from G. T. Construction."

Ana was shocked. She had no idea that Garrett was a contractor. "Garrett's in the construction business?"

Vance nodded. "There wouldn't be any reason for you to know. He's only been back the past few years, just part-time until his father got ill and Garrett had to make the move permanent."

Ana shook her head. "I guess I haven't been keeping up on the town news."

"Is it a problem? I mean, with Josie and their past together?"

Ana shrugged. "My sister lives in L.A. Why would she care if Garrett did the work or not? Especially if we get a good deal. Will we get a good deal?"

"We can cut costs if we do a lot of the work ourselves, and contract out only what we need to have done."

"It's still going to cost a lot of money, isn't it?"

"That's why we need to go to the bank," he said. "We have an appointment at one o'clock on Friday with the loan officer, Alan Hoffman."

"So we're really going to do this?"

"I thought you wanted to, Ana."

"I do. It's just a big step, and what if we fail? We'll jeopardize the ranch even more."

"The ranch is already in trouble, and if we don't bring in more revenue it will be taken away. Tomorrow, Garrett is stopping by to go over the plans and the cost. If you feel it's too much, then we can come up with something else."

Vance took her hand and squeezed it. "I would never ask you to do something that made you uncomfortable. And we'll run it all past your sisters, too."

Ana nodded. How could she not love this man, when he worked so hard to make sure she was included in everything? "What about Colt?"

"I mentioned some of this today during my visit, but of course he didn't say anything. I would like to take the plans to show him, if you and your sisters agree to the idea."

It was hard to keep her focus on business when all she wanted to do was kiss the man. "So is the business portion of this date over?"

He frowned, then a smile stretched across his handsome face as he placed her hand on his thigh. "Yes. We can finish any business tomorrow. I have other plans for the rest of the night."

"You do? Care to share?"

He lowered his head and his voice. "Oh, darlin', if I told you what I'm thinking about doing to you, you might run for the hills."

She looked into his dark eyes. "I doubt that. In fact, I have a few ideas of my own."

* * *

Two hours later, Vance helped Ana out of the truck at the house. He was a little nervous as they walked up the steps and went inside. The house was quiet, and he knew Kathleen had already retired to her residence off the kitchen. She had left a light on in the hallway.

"I guess Kathleen has already gone to bed," Ana said. "I could make some coffee, or something else if you want."

He could tell she was as nervous as he was. He turned her toward him. "Ana, I don't want to put any pressure on you. Last night was incredible, but that doesn't mean I take for granted that there will be a repeat."

Her large eyes locked on his. "What if I want a…repeat?"

He reached for her and pulled her against him. "I'd say I'm a pretty lucky guy."

She smiled. "Then that also makes me a lucky girl."

He couldn't kiss her, because he would never get her upstairs. "Maybe we should finish this discussion in the bedroom."

Vance took Ana's hand, loving the feeling of her beside him, making him think of the possibility of a future together. Once inside his bedroom, he stopped and kissed her, long and deep.

"I want you, Ana." His breathing was labored. "I also want you to know that I care about you, too. A lot. I've never felt this way about anyone before. When we get through this with Colt and the ranch…"

He shivered as she placed tiny kisses along his jaw. "You're talking too much, Vance." She started to unbutton his shirt. "Just show me," she challenged him.

He walked her toward the bed and paused to look down on the beautiful woman before him. "I don't think there's enough time, or the words to say how you make me feel."

"No words, Vance. Make love to me."

His mouth closed over hers and all worries were put aside for another time. This was all about them.

CHAPTER ELEVEN

THE NEXT AFTERNOON in the ranch office with Vance and Garrett, Ana studied the building plans laid out on the large desk.

She turned to Garrett. "I'm surprised by how quickly you came up with a design, and a very impressive one."

He smiled. "I have a good team."

Garrett Temple was a handsome man, with his nearly black hair and gray eyes. Just a little shorter then Vance, he was still over six feet. He and Ana had been in the same class in school, but back then he'd only had eyes for Josie. The pair broke up when they both went to different colleges.

"So you like the design?" Garrett asked.

She suddenly realized she hadn't said anything. "Oh, yes. I love it. It's more than I could ask for, but it's the cost that worries me."

Garret directed her attention to the construction bid. "This cost includes the large main structure and also six one-bedroom cabins. As I explained to Vance, we'll be able to complete the exterior of the main building, also do the rough electrical and plumbing before the bad weather sets in. I broke down the costs for that. And I'll leave the option open for the cabins until the spring."

Ana studied the amount they needed to begin. She knew

they were getting a great deal, but it was still a lot. "I appreciate this, Garrett, but I'm not sure we can come up with the money."

Vance finally made his presence known. "Ana, we're going to see Hoffman at the bank on Friday. We could get a construction loan."

"Or you could get a partner," Garrett added. "This is a sound investment. Something I'd seriously consider investing in."

Oh, boy, Josie would love that. Her ex-boyfriend helping them save the ranch. "Not that we don't appreciate the offer, Garrett, but I'm not sure a partnership is something we're looking for right now." She wanted to be honest. "And there's Colt. We haven't discussed this new idea with him."

Garrett slowly nodded, as if he realized she was thinking about Josie. "Okay, I'll leave the plans with you, and when you decide, let me know. Just don't wait too long." He picked up his hat and headed for the door, then paused and turned around. "I hope you'll consider letting me help, Ana. Don't let the past cloud your decision. I'd hate to see you lose everything."

"I don't want that, either, Garrett. I'm doing everything to keep that from happening."

Would Josie feel that way, too?

That afternoon, Vance left Ana in the office, talking on the phone with her sisters, while he went back to work. Hours later, when he came in from the barn, she was still in there. "Hey, this isn't good," he said as he walked into the office. "You can't keep working like this."

"I just got off the phone with Josie. I had to send her a copy of the plans."

He crossed the room, pulled Ana to her feet and brushed

a kiss across her mouth. He didn't miss how tired she looked. "Well, now it's time to stop for the night and eat some supper."

"I'm not really hungry. I think I'll just go upstairs to my room."

He didn't like that idea. "First you eat." He escorted her to the kitchen, where Kathleen had beef stew simmering in the Crock-Pot, and fresh biscuits.

Ana went to her place at the table and sat down. "Okay, maybe I'll have a little."

The housekeeper smiled. "That's my girl." She set a bowl in front of her and Ana dug into her food.

Vance concentrated on his meal, too, since she didn't seem to be interested in anything but the stew. Had something happened since the meeting?

They finished supper and Ana carried her bowl to the sink. "If you don't mind, I'm going up to bed. I'm exhausted. Good night." She walked out of the kitchen.

Vance watched her depart, a little hurt that she didn't even acknowledge him outside of being polite.

Kathleen brought two mugs of coffee to the table. "She's carrying a lot on her shoulders right now, so don't take it personally."

"Can't she let me help her?" he said, unable to keep the frustration out of his voice.

The housekeeper frowned. "Our Ana is independent. All the girls are for that matter. Blame Colt for her being so leery about trusting. She needs a man to treat her like she matters. Be honest with her, Vance, and the trust will come." Kathleen smiled. "She'll know your true feelings."

Be honest. That was the problem; he hadn't been completely honest with Ana. He needed to fix that and fast.

After helping Kathleen with the dishes, he went upstairs. He walked by Ana's room and paused, but decided to shower first and come up with a way to tell her about the land Colt had given him.

Fifteen minutes later, he slipped on a pair of pajama bottoms and made his way to the room across the hall from the bathroom. Did she want to step back from what was growing between them? He refused to let her shut him out, not until he said what he had to say. He needed to have everything out in the open.

He knocked on the door, then didn't wait for an invitation, but walked in. She was already in bed, looking over more papers.

"Vance." She said his name in the breathy way that caused his body to tighten with need.

He walked to the bed and took the papers from her, then set them on the night table.

"Vance, I'm still making notes."

"Not tonight, Ana." He sat down on the edge of the mattress, facing her, then leaned closer and covered her mouth in a tender kiss. "You said you needed to rest, but you're not resting." He kept teasing those sweet lips until she finally moaned and wrapped her arms around his neck.

"What do you have in mind?" she whispered, taking her own nibbles.

"I thought I could help you…relax." He pulled her to him, craving her closeness as much as his next breath. His body tightened with need for her. "I give a great back rub, or whatever else you have in mind." He began to demonstrate, and she soon was making purring sounds as his hands stroked slowly over her back.

"Oh, Vance, that feels wonderful," she moaned. "You can stop in about a hundred years."

He smiled. He wanted a lifetime with her, too. "Ana, we need to talk." He stopped the movement of his hands and pulled her against him.

"Okay." She dropped her head on his shoulder.

"About five years ago, I graduated college."

She yawned. "I know. Kathleen told me."

"First of all, I want you to know it wasn't my idea. Colt bribed me, because he knew how badly I wanted my own place someday. So he said he would give me some land if I got my degree. When I did, he deeded me three sections of the ranch. I've planted alfalfa on two of those sections. The third is the north meadow." He paused. "It's your magic meadow."

Tense, he waited for Ana's reaction, but there was none. Then he heard the soft sound of her breathing, which told him she had fallen asleep.

He closed his eyes as his head fell against the bedframe. What should he do now? Wake her up, make her listen to his confession again?

He'd tell her tomorrow. He reached over the shut off the light, then slid down in the bed and pulled Ana against him. He had to make this right, because he didn't want to think about how hurt she would be when she found out.

Ana shifted in his arms. "Vance," she breathed. "I'm glad you're here."

He pressed a kiss on her lips and knew that he'd never have to give her up. "So am I, bright eyes, so am I."

Friday afternoon, at five minutes to one, Vance pulled the truck into the bank parking lot. He turned off the engine and looked at Ana. He saw the worry on her face as she continued to glance over the loan application. Nothing he'd said or done over the past few days could ease her fears.

He reached across the bench seat, unfastened her safety belt and pulled her to him. "Ana, stop worrying. It's going to be fine."

"I can't help it, Vance. This income is crucial."

"Then let me help. You don't need to do everything yourself."

She laid her head against his shoulder. "Sorry, I haven't been the best company."

He took her hand, raised it to his mouth and kissed her fingers. "You can be as grumpy as you like. Just don't turn away from me. I want to share the good and the bad with you."

She nodded.

"No matter what happens today, we'll figure out another way to go," he said, trying to reassure her. "Do you believe me?"

She raised her sapphire gaze to meet his and smiled.

"That's my girl." He pulled her into a tight embrace, loving the feeling of her closeness. He kissed the side of her face along her jaw, moving slowly toward her tempting mouth, but resisted. "I think we better get out of the truck before we draw a crowd."

Vance opened the cab door and blew out a breath to calm his thundering heart. He walked around to the passenger side, trying to tamp down his fears about getting this loan. It wasn't only for the ranch, but for a future with Ana. Something they could build on together.

He wanted more than just to be the kid who'd always been looking in from the outside. He wanted to be her partner, and not only at running the Lazy S.

Ana got out of the truck and began to walk toward the bank, feeling Vance's reassuring hand at the small of her back. She was glad he was with her. Funny, how much her life had changed. A few months ago she'd been content in her career at the high school. Her life had been predicable and a little boring.

Now she couldn't imagine living away from the ranch, away from Vance. Life without him, not seeing him every day. That could happen if they didn't pull this off. She felt his strength next to her, and it helped boost her courage.

She released a long breath as they walked into Royerton First National Bank. The building was over a hundred years old, and not much had changed on the inside. She hoped their view on loaning money to women had.

Vance directed her to the reception desk, where a young woman, a onetime student of hers, Cari Petersen, was waiting for them. "Hello, Ms. Slater."

"Hi, Cari." They exchanged some pleasantries, but her nervousness didn't subside. "Is Mr. Hoffman in?"

The girl nodded. "He's expecting you." She raised the phone to her ear and announced them. Then she stood and escorted them down the hall, where they were surprised to find Alan Hoffman Jr. waiting for them. He'd gone to school with Ana, too. Wasn't he too young to hold this position, make these decisions? She'd thought they would see his father.

"Hello, Ana, Mr. Rivers."

They shook hands, and then he escorted them into the large paneled office and directed them to the chairs in front of the desk. Alan took his seat behind it.

"First of all," he began, "how is your father doing?"

"He's recovering nicely, thank you," Ana said. "He should be home soon, in fact."

Alan grinned. "My dad will be happy to hear that. Colt is one of our favorite customers."

"One of the reasons we're here," Ana began, "is because we want to keep the Lazy S solvent." She rushed on to say, "There have been some rough years with the economy, so we'd like to expand the family business. I believe you have our proposal in front of you."

They sat and waited as the banker skimmed over everything and asked several questions about the project.

Vance gave a pitch about their profits with just the limited business so far.

Alan took off his glasses and leaned back in his chair. "This all looks good on paper, but money has been tight the last few years. New businesses have come and gone with this economy." He glanced at Ana. "Are you planning on using the ranch as collateral?"

Ana froze. She'd been afraid of this; she couldn't risk the ranch, especially since they could possibly lose their leased grazing land. "That's a consideration. Of course, I will have to discuss that with my father before I do anything."

Alan nodded. "I understand. Let me present this to the loan board and get back to you."

All three stood. Alan turned to Vance. "Mr. Rivers, have you ever thought about selling any part of your land?"

Ana turned to him. Vance owned property?

Vance shook his head. "Sorry. I have plans for those sections."

"Well, if you ever change your mind, I might know of a development group who would pay top dollar for that sweet piece of meadow acreage."

Vance's face paled. "Like I said, it's not for sale."

What meadow? *Her* meadow? Ana's heart sank and she suddenly felt sick. Somehow she managed to hold it together until they were out of the building. Then she took off down the street. She could hear Vance calling her name, but Ana didn't stop. She couldn't breathe.

All these years she'd done everything to be the perfect daughter but her father had never wanted her. Why would he, when he had Vance?

Her long stride ate up the distance along the sidewalk as she headed for her apartment. She needed to be alone. Someplace where she could deal with the pain, the hurt. She felt Vance's hand on her arm and she turned around.

His gaze was intense. "Ana, talk to me."

"It's a little late for that, don't you think?"

He didn't budge. "I'm not going away until we talk."

"Well, you're going to have a long wait."

"This isn't going to solve anything, Ana. I'm either going to speak to you right here or we go someplace private."

Ana saw the curious looks of people passing by. She smiled at them in greeting. "Okay. My apartment is three blocks away."

With a nod, Vance fell into step beside her, but he remained silent as they made their way to Elk Drive. She went up the steps to her one-bedroom apartment and took out her key.

Vance knew he had to explain, but he seriously doubted he could find the right words to convince Ana he wasn't trying to take over the ranch.

He followed her into a small room that included both a living and kitchen area. Hardwoods covered the floors and the furniture was in earth tones. He glanced around the generic apartment and realized just how isolated Ana's life must be.

He stopped in the middle of the living room. "I'm sorry, Ana. I never meant for you to find out this way. Colt deeded me a few sections after I graduated from college three years ago. I tried to tell you the other night, but you fell asleep."

She didn't look convinced. "That was convenient for you."

"It's the truth. I never meant to deceive you. A month ago, I didn't think you'd care. It wasn't until we went riding to the meadow that I realized that wasn't true."

She wouldn't look at him in the eye. "Who else knows

about the land transfer? Am I the only one in town who was kept in the dark?"

"No one knew, except Wade and whoever else Colt told."

She was silent for a long time.

"Colt probably wouldn't have done it if any of his girls ever came back to the ranch."

"You have to feel welcome to want to come back." Vance could see Ana was fighting tears. "It's still our heritage," she told him. "Not yours."

Her jab hit him hard, but this time it came from someone who truly mattered to him. Right when he was beginning to think he could be a part of her life.

"Dammit, Ana, I can't change what happened over twenty years ago. I'm sorry as hell that your mother took off and left you. And I'm also sorry that Colt wasn't there for you. But I won't take the blame for it. I worked hard to make my place on the Lazy S, but I never tried to take anything away from you or your sisters."

This time her eyes were ablaze. "You didn't have to— it was given to you. You truly became the son Colt always wanted."

Vance tried to block out the hurt from her words. It didn't work this time, despite years of practice. He'd already lost, when all he'd wanted was to love her.

Two hours later, at the ranch, Vance saddled up Rusty and led his horse out of the barn. He climbed onto the chestnut cutting horse and rode across the corral. He needed to clear his head, to clear his heart of the one woman he could never have in his life.

Once through the gate, he kicked the animal's sides and the race was on. Rusty loved to run, and Vance wanted to get to a place where the hurt didn't reach him any longer. Problem was, he wasn't sure he could run that far.

Run from the mother who'd never wanted him, or a father who had no use for him except as a punching bag. Twenty years later, he still hadn't been able to outrun his past.

The river came into view and Vance suddenly realized how far he'd gone. He slowed his horse, then stopped when he saw another rider standing by a black gelding at the riverbank. Garrett.

He climbed down. "Hey, Garrett, what are you doing here?"

"I'm doing some surveying for the building. You here to chase me off Slater land?" he said jokingly.

Vance shook his head. "I have no authority to do that. But you might be wasting your time. The bank wasn't very receptive about the project."

Garrett tipped his hat back as their horses drank from the river. "Then find another source for the money."

Vance wasn't in the mood to talk about this. "I doubt Ana is interested anymore."

Garrett tied his horse's reins to a branch of a tree and leaned against the truck. "What happened? You two have a lovers' quarrel?"

Vance head shot up. "How...?"

His friend laughed. "You're not good at hiding much, Rivers. Whenever Ana comes around you get all tense and can't take your eyes off her." He sobered. "I take it she's the one you want to share that new house of yours with."

Vance froze. Now that the words were spoken, it made him realize how crazy he'd been to even think they could have a future together. "You have those designs finished already?"

Garrett gave a nod. "Take some advice and show them to her before you break ground. A woman wants to add her own touches."

"The way things look now, I need to hold off on thinking about anything permanent."

His friend studied him a second. "That serious, huh?"

He nodded in turn. "Thanks to Colt, Ana isn't going to ever trust me again."

Garrett shook his head. "I know that feeling all too well."

Vance saw the strange look on his friend's face. The man had his own past troubles with a Slater woman.

"I'm not a good one to ask for help with your love life, but I might have some ideas about the business side," Garrett stated.

Vance knew that was pretty much all he had left. He needed to concentrate on the ranch, and leave anything personal out of it. Could he do that? Could he give up on the woman he'd loved all these years? It seemed Ana had already answered that question for him.

The next afternoon Vance stormed into Colt's room, to find him sitting by the window.

"Colt, you need to do something," he said. "To start with, you can't keep letting Ana or any of your daughters think that you don't care about them."

"What h-happened?"

Vance paced the room. He hated that he had to do this when the man was still recovering, but everything was falling apart.

"What didn't happen? Ana has been trying to come up with a way to pay off the lease." He went on to explain about the idea for bringing in more revenue. He told Colt about the plans for building cabins to bring in more anglers. Not knowing if there was still animosity between the Slaters and the Temples, he conveniently left out that Garrett was heading up the project.

"Whether you like the idea or not, the Lazy S needs to make money, and Ana and her sisters have been working hard to make that happen. She needs some encouragement from you."

Colt frowned. He hadn't seen Ana in the past two days, but thought that was because she'd been busy. She had told him some things about the project and he had enjoyed hearing her enthusiasm. Something wasn't right between her and Vance. "What d-did you d-do?"

The younger man stopped and glared at him. "What did I do? I did nothing. You're the one who teamed me up with Ana to run the place, when it should have been your daughters in charge. I'm an outsider. Not family."

Colt hesitated. Was that how Vance felt? "You know the r-ranch."

Vance sent him another glare. "And whose fault is that? Your daughters would like to know how the ranch runs, but you refused to show them."

Colt fought not to look away.

"I watched for years how you treated them," Vance said. "How you barely acknowledged them. Why, Colt? What did they do that was so wrong?"

Colt was ashamed of his lousy parenting. After Luisa left, he'd wallowed in self-pity, ignoring the girls until they stopped depending on him for anything. It had been easier that way. He wouldn't be hurt again when they left.

"Do you know that Ana can't trust another man because you've never been there for her?" Vance crouched down in front of his chair. "Ana feels lost, Colt. She's hurt because of the land you deeded to me. Now she hates me because she thinks I matter more to you than she does. And I don't blame her. But unlike you, I care about her."

Colt's chest ached. He hadn't wanted this to happen.

"So you can't hide any longer. You need to tell her the

truth. Let her know how you feel before it's too late." Vance turned and walked out of the room, leaving Colt alone.

He sat there in the deafening silence. Was this what his life had become? He'd pushed just about everyone who ever care about him away. Maybe he deserved to lose everything and to end up a lonely old man.

Memories flooded into his head. The good ones early on, then years and years of bad memories. Years when he could have made a better life for his girls, but had chosen not to. He'd stood back and let someone else care for them; someone else got Ana's, Tori's, Josie's and Marissa's kisses and hugs. Someone else got their love.

He brushed a tear from his face. "It's your own damn fault, old man," he chided himself, not wanting to go back to that life. He wanted Ana to stay at the ranch, and try and bring the other girls home, too.

He turned his wheelchair and reached for the phone on his bedside table. He got the operator. "I need the R-Royerton First National Bank." He waited until a woman's voice answered. "Alan H-Hoffman Sr."

"Who's calling, sir?"

"C-Colton Slater," he said. Although the effort was exhausting, his speech was clear.

Hoffman's booming voice came over the line. "Well, you old son of a gun, how are you?"

Colt smiled, hearing the familiar voice. "B-better. N...need a favor, friend."

"Okay. What's going on?" Sarah stepped into Ana's apartment two days later.

It was after ten o'clock in the morning, but Ana hadn't showered or gotten dressed yet. "What are you talking about?" She shut the door behind her friend.

"Why are you staying here instead of the ranch? Don't

you usually have a hundred things to do out there? Dad said the fishing has been incredible. Word has gotten around and the anglers are asking to go out to your place."

Ana hadn't been back to the ranch since Friday. Besides not being able to face Vance, she didn't have her car.

"They're taken care of," she said. "I'm sure Vance can handle anything that comes along."

Sarah studied her. "Speaking of that good-looking man, you two seemed to be getting pretty chummy."

She wasn't that surprised by her friend's observation. "How did you know?"

Sarah smiled. "So you are dating?"

Ana shook her head and headed for the small apartment kitchen. "No. I'm not sure if we really ever were." She began to fill the coffeemaker. "I mean, we were so busy with the ranch and Dad. We just kind of fell together."

"But it was getting serious, right?"

Ana couldn't talk about it. "Not anymore. I mean, it never was. I should have stayed focused on the ranch and taking care of Colt." She leaned against the counter. "Then it wouldn't hurt so much."

"Oh, honey, I can't believe Vance doesn't care about you."

Ana shook her head. "No, but it doesn't change the fact that he's always had Colt's attention."

"And you blame Vance for that?"

Ana looked at her friend and brushed her hair away from her face. "No. Yes. I don't know."

"I do," Sarah said. "Vance was only a kid when he showed up. Okay, Colt took him in, but I bet whatever Vance got from your father he earned with hard work."

"What about me, Tori, Josie and Marissa?" Ana knew she sounded like a spoiled child. "Don't we deserve anything?"

"Of course you do. And isn't it about time to finally confront Colt about this issue?"

Ana's bravado began to fade. "But what if he finally tells me the truth? What if he tells me that he doesn't love me?"

CHAPTER TWELVE

OVER THE NEXT week Vance tried to stay busy with the day-to-day running of the ranch, but all he could think about was Ana. Then to top it off he'd gotten a call from Hoffman at the bank, who asked to see him. Vance called Ana, but she didn't answer, so all he could do was leave a message telling her about their appointment.

He wasn't surprised when he walked into the bank lobby and she wasn't there. Not that he expected her to be able to forgive him, but he had hoped that they could at least work together for the ranch. He'd thought wrong.

He walked into Alan's office and was greeted by a smile. "Hello, Vance. Good to see you again."

Vance hoped the man was feeling this good for a reason. They exchanged handshakes.

"Glad you could come in. Will Ana be joining us?"

"She couldn't make it today," Vance said. "I'll relay any news to her."

"That's right, the school year is starting soon." The loan officer looked over the papers on his desk. "Well then, I guess you'll get the pleasure of telling her the good news. We've approved the loan."

"You're giving us the business loan?"

Alan nodded. "Yes, and for the amount requested. I have

the paperwork right here. Since you're partners, I'll need Ana's signature, too."

"Of course." Vance was caught off guard by the news.

"We could get your signature today, and if you take the papers to Ana to look over, she can return them at her leisure." Alan smiled. "Just have her call to arrange a time to come in and sign. We need to make sure it's notarized."

The banker sobered. "Vance, about the other day, I overstepped when I mentioned your property. From Ana's expression, I take it she didn't know that Colt had deeded it over to you."

Vance nodded. He remembered Alan Hoffman from high school, but they hadn't been friends. Not with his father being the bank manager. Many parents didn't let their boys associate with that good-for-nothing Rivers kid. "I was surprised when he gave it to me."

Alan held up his hands. "You worked hard for Colton over the years. If he's anything like my father, you earned every acre."

Vance shrugged. "I only did my job."

"I'd say you did a lot more than that."

"You mean despite being Calvin Rivers's son?"

"Okay, we all knew of your dad's reputation, but I hope you know we're not looking back. The people in this town respect you, Vance. You made a place for yourself in this community."

Vance should be happy with this man's praise, but without Ana none of it mattered to him. "Thank you."

Hoffman nodded. "So that being said, I do know of a buyer for your land if you're interested."

Vance thought back to the day he'd ridden to the meadow with Ana. He could still hear the wonder in her voice as she'd looked over the land of her ancestors. "Sorry, it's not for sale." He took the loan papers, said his good-byes and walked out.

Once outside of the bank, Vance stood on the sidewalk. What was his next move? So far, he'd lost the most important thing to him—Ana. No matter what he planned to do with the land, she wouldn't give him a chance to tell her.

He walked two blocks to the office of Wade Dickson, Attorney at Law. Vance removed his hat and walked inside to the receptionist's desk. "Hello, Mrs. Smart. Is Wade in?"

The middle-aged woman smiled. "I'll see, Vance." She went to the door, knocked, then peered inside. After an exchange of words, she motioned for Vance to go in.

He walked into the office. Before the lawyer could even stand, Vance stated his case. "I need some advice."

Wade made an effort not to smile. "Ana?"

He nodded.

"Have you tried to tell her how you feel about her?"

Vance wished he had the chance. "I don't think any amount of sweet words are going to fix this."

After trying for the past two days, Vance didn't know where else to go to look for Ana. The only place left was the high school, since classes were starting the following Monday. It might be his best shot to catch her.

Memories flooded back as he walked through the double doors and down the hall to the main office. As a fourteen-year-old, he'd spent a lot of time with the principal before Colt had given him a home and adjusted his bad attitude.

A woman coming out of an inner office told him where Ana's office was, and he set out on a search. He walked the short distance to the counseling center, where he spotted her right away.

Through the glass partition he could see she was busy

talking with another teacher. She wore her dark hair pulled back in a ponytail, with short bangs across her forehead.

He zeroed in on those big eyes that had mesmerized him for years. No wonder blue was his favorite color. Ana blue. He shifted his gaze to her full mouth, and quickly his hunger grew.

The sight of her delicate jaw and long slender neck had him recalling how he'd trailed kisses down her body, raising goose bumps on her heated skin. He treasured the memories of their nights together, with her pressed so close to him. How she'd given herself so freely, never asking for anything back. Yet he wanted all of her.

Ana raised her gaze to his, her cobalt eyes as cold and unwelcoming as a mountain stream. She didn't look happy to see him. Somehow he had to change that, get her to forgive him.

She said something to the other person, then walked out into the hall. "Vance. What are you doing here?"

"You wouldn't take my calls, so I came here to see you."

"That's because we have nothing to talk about."

It hurt that she could so easily ignore what they had. "Yes, we do, Ana." He took a step toward her. "So either we discuss it here or go inside to your office. But we're going to talk."

Ana worked to stay calm, hating that Vance could cause such a reaction in her. She didn't need to spend any time with him. She still hurt. She might never get over his deception.

She moved away from the doorway and let him inside. She closed the door, though there wasn't much privacy, which was a good thing. So why did it feel so intimate?

He sat down in the only chair besides hers, and she caught his familiar scent, a mixture of soap and pure Vance.

He placed an envelope on her desk. "It's the loan papers."

"Loan papers?"

"The bank came through with our building loan."

She tried not to appear surprised. "They're giving us the money?"

Vance nodded. "And since we're still joint executors of Colt's estate, we need to make a decision. Do we move ahead with the lodge?"

Ana didn't know what to do. She hadn't told her sisters any more because she'd doubted they were going to get the loan. "I need to talk to Tori, Josie and Marissa."

He nodded. "What about Colt? He's still head of the family."

She stared, openmouthed. Had they really been a real family? She was more doubtful now than ever before.

It took two days before Ana got the nerve to go to the rehab center and see her father. She thought it would be better to wait until some of her anger subsided. There had been so much hurt over the years, but nothing compared to this. Every glimmer of hope she'd had these past weeks about reconciling with her dad began to fade away. She had to let it go.

She blinked back the tears as she made her way down the hall to his room, knowing this discussion should have happened years ago. It was time to figure out where she stood with the man. She wasn't going to beg Colt Slater for his love.

She knocked on the door and looked inside. Colt was seated in his wheelchair, staring out the window. She felt her pulse pounding and her stomach tighten, but she refused to leave. They had to deal with this problem.

Colt was a handsome man for his age. Of course, fifty-four wasn't old by most standards. His rough-cut jaw was cleanshaven and his thick graying hair trimmed neatly. His eyes were deep set and a brilliant blue. His shoulders and chest were broad and his stomach flat. She had no doubt that the ex-rodeo star could still attract women.

Ana crossed the room, sat down in the chair beside him and glanced at the view of the Rocky Mountains. The two of them sat in silence for a few seconds, then Ana said, "We got the loan to start building the lodge and cabins."

She threw it out there to see how her father would react, good or bad.

"Good."

She was a little surprised. Colt had always been a private man. He'd never wanted anyone on his land.

"So you're okay with this business venture? There will be anglers and other guests on the ranch."

He nodded.

"You want me to go ahead with this?"

Colt turned and looked at her. "Y-yes, Ana, I w-want you there v-very much."

She blinked, surprised at the clarity of his speech. "You're talking."

He nodded again.

"How long?"

"It's b-been getting b-better every day."

She smiled. "Oh, Tori and Josie and Marissa are going to be so happy."

He shook his head. "No, p-please don't tell them. Y…yet."

"Why?"

"They won't c-come back."

Ana was confused. "You want them to come home?"

There was a flash of sadness in his eyes before he glanced away. "'Cause, I m-miss you all."

Ana felt angry, though tears gathered in her eyes. She

shook her head in disbelief. "No, don't say that if you don't mean it."

Her father reached for her hand. She could feel the strength, the calluses on the pads of his fingers. "I m-made m-mistakes. I need to fix them."

Part of her wanted to run, but the other wanted to embrace this man. "Why now? You never seemed to want us around when we were growing up. We did everything to try and please you, but it wasn't enough. It was never enough." She jumped up and moved to the other side of the room. "And now you suddenly want us to act like we're one big, happy family."

"No!" he said, his voice strong. "I w-want to make it up to you." He held her gaze. But there was so much emotion showing on his face she had to look away. Why was he doing this to her?

"Ana, I'm s-sorry. I wasn't the f-father I sh-should have been to you girls. Please give me a second ch-chance to make it up to you."

Her chest hurt so badly she couldn't breathe, but Ana wasn't about to cry. The last thing she needed was to let him see how much she cared that he'd finally said the words she'd ached to hear all those years. Could she forgive him? Would her sisters? She pushed that aside as more hurt surfaced.

"If you loved us so much, why did you give away our land to Vance?"

Colt looked startled by her words. "Ana...I—"

"No, don't say anything." She waved her hand. "I've got to go," she said, and hurried from the room. She didn't want to deal with any of the men in her life.

The next day, Ana realized she couldn't handle everything on her own. She picked up the phone in the ranch office and called her sisters.

"Slater Style," Josie answered.

"Hi, Josie, it's Ana."

"Hey, I was about to call you. Wait, let me get Tori and put you on speakerphone."

After about thirty seconds, Ana's other sister came on board. "Okay, Ana, tell us what's going on," she said. "You have any news from the bank?"

Ana was sad that they hadn't asked about their father. That was when she realized that telling them of his speedy improvement wouldn't bring them home anytime soon. And that was top priority.

"Yes, they approved our loan."

There was a pause, then Josie said, "That's great. So when do you and Vance break ground on the project?"

"I'm working with Vance as little as possible."

"Wait a minute," Josie began. "I thought you and he were the ones Colt put in charge."

Ana wasn't sure she wanted to tell them about the land. "Let's just say we disagree on a lot of things. That doesn't mean we can't go ahead with this project."

"Are you sure?" Josie asked, concern in her voice.

"Yes, G. T. Construction is ready to break ground next week." Ana prayed her sisters wouldn't ask any questions about the contractor. "We can't delay it much longer or we'll run into bad weather. I want you all involved with this."

There was silence again and Ana knew the twins were trying to decide what to say next. "How involved do you need us to be?" Tori asked.

"I'll appreciate any and all of your input and support, because there will be a lot more decisions to make. Next week, I go back full-time to my job at the high school. I won't be here 24/7 to oversee things."

"Wait a minute," Tori interrupted. "What about Vance? He'll be around, won't he?"

Ana closed her eyes and released a breath. "Yes, he's here, but he's also busy with the ranch business. Right now, he's cutting the alfalfa crop." She released another breath, relieved he wasn't around. She'd seen him on the mower in the field when she drove out to the ranch this morning.

"Isn't he going to help you supervise this project?" Josie asked.

Ana wasn't sure of much anymore. "Vance will be acting as the ranch foreman. That's his job. I'll oversee things with the contractor."

"So you can handle this by yourself?"

"I don't have a choice. We need the revenue or we lose the ranch, and we all agreed that this was a good way to bring in more money. Even Colt agrees."

"Colt?" Josie said. "How did you get him to agree with the idea?"

That had been more of a courtesy than their father had given her when he deeded away Slater land. "I just told him something needed to be done." Ana couldn't help but think about how much of an improvement he'd made. "Speaking of our dad, he'll be released from the rehab center and be coming home soon. That means we have to think about hiring some help, or one of you needs to come home."

That got the twins stammering about how their businesses needed their full attention at the moment. They promised they would take it up with their youngest sister.

Ana finally let them off the hook and told them she would handle things. After she hung up the phone, she realized what a job she'd taken on. And unlike before, she would be handling it alone.

She got to her feet, deciding she was hungry. It was already after one o'clock and she needed some nourishment to face her meeting with Garrett. She walked into the kitchen, expecting to find Kathleen, but instead saw Vance looking in the refrigerator.

With him in that position she got a good look at the jeans pulled tightly over his rear end. His shirt was sweat streaked and clinging to his muscular back. Her pulse started racing and her mouth went dry. Great. All she needed was an out-of-control libido.

She'd started to back out of the room when he turned around with his arms full of sandwich makings. He raised his dark eyes to hers. Then, surprisingly, he smiled at her.

"Hi."

"Hi. I was looking for Kathleen," she fibbed. "Is she around?"

"She's off today. If it's important, she's at her sister's in town." He put everything down on the counter. "Can I help you with something?" He came around the island and crossed to her.

Ana refused to back up. "No, thank you. I'm handling it." She decided to change the subject. "I saw you cutting the alfalfa."

He nodded. "I think the crop should bring in enough money to cover the rest of the lease money."

She shook her head. "It's not all Slater land. Part of that crop is yours, since it's on one of your sections."

He shook his head. "No matter what's on paper, Ana, it goes into the same pot."

She didn't want to discuss this. "Were you planning to be here as foreman all your life?"

Vance couldn't get enough of looking at Ana. He'd missed her over the past few days. "No. I was going to have my own place."

"And I expect you to continue with those plans. You

have your land and your crop. I'd say that's a pretty good start on a new life."

Her rejection hurt. Ana had that power over him, especially now that she'd given him a glimpse of a life he'd only dreamed about.

Well, she wasn't going to walk away from something they both wanted, without feeling what he was feeling. He took a step closer to her and inhaled her sweetness. "Sometimes things that seem perfect are far from it, especially when no matter what you do, you still can't have the most important thing."

He reached for her and drew her against him, causing her to gasp. He took advantage of that and covered her mouth with his. In an instant the heat was turned up. He had this one chance to let her know what a good thing they had. He cupped her face and tilted her head so he could deepen the kiss. When she breathed a sigh, his tongue slipped into her mouth, tasting her addicting sweetness.

Ana's arms slipped around his waist in surrender to the kiss, and he took advantage again, pressing his body against hers. He was fighting dirty, but he was about to lose everything. This was all he had.

She finally broke off the kiss with another gasp. He looked down at her eyes, laced with desire. He could continue the seduction, but she'd only end up hating him more. He had to walk away or lose his mind.

"Goodbye, Ana." Vance turned and headed out the door. He didn't need to be hit over the head to realize how crazy it was to think he could fit into her life. He'd always be the kid who was outside looking in, looking for a place to belong.

CHAPTER THIRTEEN

THE NEXT DAY started out with problems. Ana not only thought about Vance most of the night, she overslept, and had to begin her morning rushing to her appointment at the bank to sign papers. When she finally arrived, she found Wade waiting for her. Her father's lawyer explained that he was taking over as executor. Vance would no longer be her partner for the project.

Ana couldn't hide her surprise. Something was going on, and no one was telling her anything.

"Isn't this what you wanted?" Wade asked her.

She thought about Vance's deception, but for him to walk away... "Maybe, since I can't trust him."

When Alan walked out of the room to make copies, she asked Wade, "Why didn't you tell me Dad had given land to Vance?"

The lawyer frowned. "That choice was your father's. I'm sorry he never discussed it with you."

"But those sections were an important part of the ranch."

Wade gave her a confused look. "That may be, Ana, but they were Colt's to give away. And although your father recently had a stroke and is *temporarily* incapable of running the operation, he had every right back then to deed that land to Vance."

In her head Ana knew Wade was correct, but her heart

was broken over it. "You're right, Wade. Colt can do whatever he wants. He'll be home soon, so he can take over again."

Wade sighed. "You know, Ana, you can be as stubborn and bullheaded as your father. And I'm going to tell you the same thing I told Colt. To take this time and try to build a relationship."

Tears blurred Ana's vision. "I've tried."

Wade hugged her. "Oh, darlin', I know you have, and that old cuss is more to blame than anyone." The lawyer stepped back and she wiped her tears away. "Colt might not deserve this chance, but life is too short not to try and work this out. Not just with your dad, but with Vance."

She nodded. She didn't want to think about Vance, but her heart had other ideas.

Thirty minutes later, the loan money had been put into an escrow account so they could start the construction. So why didn't Ana feel excited about the project?

She walked outside with Wade, who hugged her again, then said, "Don't be too hard on Vance. He's a good man." He smiled. "And I think you'll learn that sooner or later. Hopefully, not too late."

Before Ana could say anything, Wade started back to his office, leaving her confused about so many things. But she had to put all that aside for now.

She walked across the street toward the Big Sky Grill for her meeting with Garrett. Then she had to return to the ranch and help set up the downstairs guest room for her father's return home. The living room needed to be stripped of furniture, which would be replaced by physical therapy equipment. Jay would come by three days a week to help with Colt's workouts.

Ana was excited and nervous about her father's homecoming. Was Wade right? Was Colt ready to build a relationship?

She walked through the door of the restaurant and a flash of memory hit her. Vance had brought her here and they'd shared a hamburger and fries like a lot of other couples. Had they been a couple? Whether they had been or not, her problem now would be to turn off her feelings for the man. Seeing him every day was going to be hard, so she hoped he'd concentrate on the cattle operation and stay out of her way.

She didn't need be reminded of what they'd had together, or what she thought they'd had. Their kisses, their nights together. She wanted to hate him, but yesterday in the kitchen he'd looked lost. She shook away any sympathy. He still had lied to her. He had to know how much she loved that section of land.

She heard her name called and looked toward the booth in the corner. She put on a smile and crossed the restaurant.

"Sorry I'm late." Ana slid into her seat "It took longer at the bank then I thought."

Garrett smiled back. "Not a problem."

He got the waitress's attention and ordered coffee. "Is everything okay with the loan?"

She nodded. "I signed all the papers, so do you want to talk about a starting date?"

"I sure do." He leaned toward her. "I can have a crew there by next week. If the weather cooperates, we can get those slabs poured before the end of the week."

Good. Colt would be arriving home then. "That fast?"

"As they say, time is money. And my guys want and need the work."

She released a breath. The way it looked, she was handling this project alone. "Okay, let's do it."

Garrett stood. "I'll have a crew there in the morning." He checked his watch, then made a quick phone call on his cell and finalized the arrangements. He hung up. "It's all set, How about some lunch to celebrate?"

"I don't want to hold you up," she said.

"You're not. In fact, if I was home right now, I'd be pacing around."

The waitress appeared and they put in an order for burgers and fries.

"You got a hot date later?" she teased.

He shook his head. "My son is coming to visit me."

Ana was caught off guard by the announcement. "I didn't know you had a son. You're married?"

Garrett shook his head slowly. "I'm no longer married. And yes, Brody is eight years old. He's coming to live with me. I'm hoping it's going to be permanent."

Ana was still caught up with Garrett having an eight-year-old son. How could that be? Garrett had been dating Josie back in high school and part of their college years before they'd suddenly broken up.

Garrett saw her questioning look. "I take it Josie never told you why we split up?"

Oh, boy. "Only that you met someone else."

"It hadn't been the wisest behavior, but my son is a result of that action. Although my marriage didn't survive, Brody is and will always be the joy of my life." Garrett studied Ana. "I hope this won't affect our business relationship."

She quickly shook her head. "No. This has nothing to do with the past. You're helping us build our future. And besides, Josie isn't going to be any more involved in this project than via phone calls. She's already made that clear to me several times."

That seemed to make Garrett relax. "Then I guess we start work on Friday."

"That sounds perfect." Ana hoped her words turned out to be true, or she could be in a lot of trouble, and not only with the ranch.

* * *

By late that afternoon, Vance had packed up most of his personal things, nearly twenty years' worth. He'd send for the rest later, because he had only so much room in his truck. He just wanted to get the hell out of there, the sooner the better.

He carried the last box outside and loaded it in the truck bed, then slammed the tailgate. He glanced around the compound and toward the big red barn where he'd first lived, in the apartment upstairs. His gaze moved to the bunkhouse, then to the corral where Rusty was prancing around, hoping someone wanted to go for a ride. Vance wished he could take his chestnut gelding with him, but for now he wasn't sure where he would be living. Would he buy some land, or find another job as foreman?

"Goodbye, fella," he called, and waited to hear the answering whinny. Then he climbed into the truck and started the engine.

He'd already said his goodbyes to the guys, and put Todd in charge of the ranch hands, knowing he'd get them to follow orders until Ana found another foreman.

Putting the truck in gear, he drove the short distance up the gravel road to the house, but followed the circular driveway until he made his way around back. He parked by the kitchen door and sat there a minute, recalling so many years ago when he'd first walked inside the Slater house. All the meals he'd shared with the family, but nothing else.

Over the years, Vance had done the work Colt gave him, and had stayed away from his daughters. He'd broken that rule recently, when Ana moved back home to help out. He must have lost his mind, because he finally admitted to himself that he had loved her all these years. He released a sigh. Well, it was past time for him to wise up. He didn't fit in here, never had.

He would leave, but not before he broke off the last tie to this place. He picked up an envelope from the seat, got out and walked up the back steps. Through the screen door he saw Kathleen at the stove, probably cooking supper.

She turned when he walked in. "Hi, Vance. You're early for supper."

"I didn't come to eat, Kathleen." He paused, then said, "I'm leaving."

She frowned. "For how long?"

He shook his head. "For good. I've already cleared my things out of the foreman's house, except for the furniture. You can keep that for the renters. Todd knows what to do for the rest of the week. The alfalfa is cut, and most of it's baled. Todd will have the men finish the job."

He kept talking, because he knew it would be too easy to change his mind. Kathleen would try to convince him to stay.

The Slaters' housekeeper had been the closest thing to a mother he'd ever known, and he never doubted that she loved him. He felt the same way about her.

"Vance Rivers, you stop this foolishness and tell me what's going on."

"It's for the best, Kathleen. I should have left here a long time ago. Ana is more than capable of handling things. She doesn't want my help." He had trouble getting the words out. "Wade can step in if she needs him. Besides, the other sisters need to pitch in, too. If I'm not here maybe they'll come back to their home."

Kathleen didn't look as if she believed any of his speech. "What about Colt? He's being released in a few days."

Vance forced a smile. He still needed to talk with Colt. "That's good. He needs to be home with his daughter. Not me."

"But you're like a son to that man. You have to know that."

Colt had been good to him, but as he did with his daughters, the man kept everyone at a distance. At the very least Vance hoped something good would come out of this and Colt would repair the relationship with his daughters. Vance needed to leave for that to happen.

"They'll never be a family with me around. I'm part of the problem. It's time, Kathleen."

Tears filled her eyes. "Where will you go?"

He sighed. "I have a place for now, but I promise I won't leave the area without saying goodbye."

He pushed away from the counter. "I'll be right back." He walked down the hall to the office, and placed the envelope on the desk. He returned to the kitchen. "I put something on the desk for Ana. Tell her…" He didn't know what to say. "Tell her I'm sorry."

"Vance, you need to tell Ana yourself. At least tell her how you feel, and fight for her."

"She doesn't want to hear anything I have to say."

"Then make her listen. If you care about her you'll stay and help her through this."

"I wish that was possible, but it's not. It's too late."

But before he could leave, he heard the front door open and close. He froze, knowing it was Ana. He started to make his exit, but Kathleen grasped his arm.

"You talk to her." Her grip tightened. "Let her know how you feel."

He shook his head. "It would never work between us." Not when Ana thought he was trying to take the ranch from her.

The sound of the footsteps caught their attention. "Is that your pot roast I smell?"

At the sound of Ana's voice, Vance tensed and started to leave, but Kathleen stopped him.

Ana walked into the kitchen, but her smile disappeared when she saw him. "Vance…"

"Ana." His gaze took her in like a starved man. Her dark hair curled around her face, but her pretty blue eyes looked tired. He started to speak and explain things, but he saw the hurt in her expression. He didn't see that anything he could say would change anything. "Look, I was just leaving. Goodbye, Ana."

He'd blown his chance with her, and now it was too late. It was time to let the dream end. He turned and walked out.

Ana could only watch as Vance left. The sound of the screen door hitting the frame made her panic, and for a split second she considered going after him. But what good would it do? If he truly cared about her wouldn't he try to work things out?

"It seems you could have talked to the man," Kathleen said. "Hear him out."

"We've tried. Vance got what he wants."

"Oh, sweetheart, if you think that then you don't know Vance as well as I thought. All he's ever wanted was to belong somewhere."

"So do I, Kathleen."

Ana fought tears as she walked out of the kitchen and down the hall to the office, where she closed the door. She could escape for now, but knew she would be seeing Vance often, even with her going back to work at the school. He would be at the house with Colt. How could she act as if everything was normal?

She walked to the desk to email her sisters about the starting date for construction. Sitting down, she saw an envelope next to the desk from Wade Dickson, Attorney at Law. What was Uncle Wade sending her? She opened the envelope and took out the papers. On top was a note.

Ana,
It was never my intention to take anything from you. You were right, the land should stay in the Slater family.
   I only hope you can convince your sisters that Lazy S is more than just land.
Good luck,
Vance

Her hand trembled as she set the note aside to glance over the papers, feeling her stomach tighten. Oh, God. It was the deed to all three sections of land, including the meadow, and they were all signed over to Analeigh Maria Slater.

Later that night, Colt was restless, so he took the offered medication to help him sleep. Lying in the dark, he still wasn't sure if going home was a good idea. He'd liked having everyone come here to visit him, but what would happen when he got back to the house? Would Ana go live in town again? He wouldn't get to see her every day like he did now.

And what about Vance? There were problems between him and Ana, Colt knew. Problems that he had created when he gave the boy part of the ranch. Colt knew why he'd done it: Vance had cared about the Lazy S, and he'd earned it.

In Colt's eyes that made it right to give him part of the place. Colt hadn't been able to take credit for much after his marriage failed, but putting Vance Rivers on a straight path had been his one shining accomplishment. He wasn't going to apologize for giving the boy the land for his dedication and hard work. Only now, it had caused more trouble.

Colt felt his eyes drifting shut and thought back to the decades of loneliness. If he had just held on to his little girls instead of pushing them away, how different things might have been for Ana, Tori, Josie and Marissa.

He brushed a tear off his face.

"Oh, Luisa," he breathed. He could still see her beautiful face when he closed his eyes. He still dreamed of her, of them together. Thought about all their hopes of a future together. But their seemingly perfect life had quickly changed when Luisa walked away.

"No puedo vivir sin ti. Te amo," he whispered in the darkness. *I can't live without you. I love you.* He'd said those words so often to his bride during their short six years together. It had been well over twenty years since they'd parted.

He fisted his hands tightly. Why hadn't he ever been able to put her completely out of his head, his heart? Why did he keep hoping she'd show up and beg him to take her back? Then he could tell her to get the hell out of his life.

"Te quiero con toda mi alma. Siempre." The female voice was a breathy whisper in the silent room. *I love you with all my soul. Always.*

Colt froze, but didn't open his eyes. He couldn't even breathe when he heard the familiar words, *"Tu eres mi vida." You are my life.*

"Luisa," he gasped, and jerked up as he glanced around the room, his eyes working to adjust to the darkness. He heard his heart pounding in his chest as he caught a faint female scent. His gaze searched every corner of the room, but found no one.

He was alone, just like always.

CHAPTER FOURTEEN

ANA SPENT THE night at the ranch, but she didn't sleep at all, not after Kathleen told her Vance had resigned and moved out of the foreman's house. Ana was haunted by the fact that she was the one who'd driven him away from his home. He'd given it all up.

Because of her.

She was ashamed that she had refused to listen to anything he had to say, and had believed the worst about him. In the end, Vance gave everything to her so she could be happy. Well, she was miserable, because he was the only thing she wanted.

Oh, God. She had to find him, to get him to stay. To make him understand that he was the one who belonged at the Lazy S. She couldn't imagine never seeing him again.

At daybreak, she began calling his cell phone. Every time, it went straight to voice mail, but she couldn't get herself to leave a message. Anything she had to say would sound so insincere. She needed to talk to Vance in person. At least to tell him she was sorry for those awful things she'd said.

She came downstairs to the kitchen to find a flurry of activity. Three ranch hands were busy moving sofas against the walls in the living room, making space for the therapy equipment being delivered in a few hours. There was a delay, and Colt wouldn't be coming home for a few more days. At least that would give Ana more time to get things together.

Todd came over to her. "It's good to see you, Ana."

"Hi, Todd," she said pleasantly.

The new foreman smiled. "I know you'll be busy, with Colt coming home and all, so if there is anything else you need, let me know."

Bring Vance back, she cried silently. "I appreciate that, Todd. I hope everything is going smoothly with the operation."

He nodded. "Of course we miss Vance, but we're handling things."

Did the men know what had happened? "Have you spoken to him?"

He nodded. "I call him when I have questions." The new foreman shrugged. "He's been here so long, no one knows the Lazy S like he does."

Ana fought her tears. "I know. I'm hoping that, with Colt coming home, things will get back to normal."

A big grin appeared on Todd's face. "The men are looking forward to the boss being home."

The young man went back to his task and Ana escaped to the kitchen, where Kathleen was busy mixing up a batch of her oatmeal raisin cookies to give the men for their help.

The housekeeper wiped her hands on her apron and came around the table. "What's wrong?"

Ana shook her head. "Oh, Kathleen, I've made a mess of everything."

"Come on, we talked about this, Ana. Your father needs to take blame for this one. In fact, he and I are going to have a long discussion when he gets home. One that I wish

I'd pushed for twenty years ago. Maybe things would have been different today."

"I don't want to rehash the past. I want to start fresh with Colt, but I'm not sure I can until I get things straightened out with Vance."

"You will, honey. Give him some time."

"No, I can't. I drove him away from his home." Ana didn't want to think of all the awful things she'd said to him. The man she cared about. The man she loved. Oh, God, she loved Vance so much. How could she have done this to him?

Kathleen led Ana to a chair at the table and sat her down. "You've had a lot to deal with since your dad's stroke. Your sisters haven't been here to help you, either. Can't blame them, though. There was a lot of resentment because of Colt's neglect. You needed someone to blame."

"You would think as an adult I would understand that what Colt did was never Vance's fault."

Kathleen sighed. "Do you think you stayed angry with Vance for another reason?"

Ana wanted to deny it, but she couldn't. She was afraid.

Kathleen smiled. "I watched for years how Vance stood back from the family, but he always had eyes for you. A crush at first, but every time you came home from college, he seemed to make excuses to show up at the house. He went through a real dark mood when you got engaged."

Ana thought back to their first kiss, when she was fourteen, and how angry he'd been with her. "I didn't think he liked me back then."

"You have to understand him. He was afraid of your father finding out. He fought to find a place to belong." Kathleen leaned forward. "To not be that kid from the wrong side of town. He's worked so hard to lose the stigma."

"Oh, God, and I put him right back there."

"No, Colt didn't handle it right. He was wrong not to tell you girls, but he wasn't wrong to give Vance part of this ranch. Don't you think the man worked hard enough to have a place where he belonged?"

Ana's heart ached. She'd messed up everything and she had to make it right. "I need to fix this, Kathleen. Please tell me where Vance is. Please tell me he didn't leave the state."

"No, he's close by." Kathleen sighed and hesitated, then said, "He's staying at Garrett's place."

"Working at the ranch?"

"No, he took a job on the construction crew."

Vance had been up since five that morning. He'd been at the lodge site, helping the men unload lumber off the flatbed truck and carry it to where the concrete slabs had been poured yesterday morning. Today they were going to frame the first floor of the structure, so there wouldn't be any break in the workload anytime soon.

He never minded hard work. It had gotten him through some rough times. Times when he hurt so badly nothing distracted him from the pain. Times when people thought he wasn't worth saving, but he'd worked to prove them wrong. Times when he loved someone so deeply that he had to bury his feelings in work.

Work wasn't doing the trick to hide what he felt for Ana. That was why he couldn't stay here.

"Hey, don't kill yourself. I have plans for you."

He looked up to see Garrett smiling at him.

Vance removed his hard hat and wiped the sweat off his forehead. "I'm only doing the job you hired me for."

Garrett motioned for him to follow him off the site.

Once under the shade of a tree, but before Garrett began to speak, Vance said, "Hey, I know I'm not as qualified as your regular guys, but I appreciate the work."

"You are qualified. In fact, my men are complaining that you're making them look bad. Slow down, Vance. Stop letting what happened between you and Ana drive you so hard you get hurt."

Vance straightened. "I'm not."

Garrett glanced over Vance's shoulder. "Well, that's good to know, because you're going to be tested on that theory." He nodded and Vance turned to see Ana walking toward them. Garrett made his exit.

Vance's chest tightened as she moved through the high grass toward him. She was in her usual attire of jeans and a blouse tucked in at her narrow waist.

"Hi, Vance," she said.

He nodded. "Ana. Is there a problem at the ranch? With Colt?"

"No, Todd is handling everything and Colt is fine." She raised her gaze to his. "I came to see you. Can we talk?"

He didn't want to rehash anything. "I really need to get back to work."

He'd started to leave when she called to him. "Please, Vance."

Her plea worked and he waited for her to speak.

"I'm sorry for all the things I said," she told him. "I took my anger out on you when I should have directed it at Dad. You have every right to the land."

He didn't want to say anything, but muttered, "You think I give a damn about that land? Well, I don't. It was never what I wanted."

Ana's eyes filled. "I know that now. And I'm sorry,

so sorry for the way I treated you." She glanced away. "I didn't trust what I was feeling for you. I got scared, Vance."

He walked a few feet away, then came back. "You don't think I wasn't scared? The problem, Ana, was you couldn't trust me. You wouldn't believe anything I said."

With her silence, all he could hear was his pulse pounding in his ears.

"I would now," she confessed.

Her words were encouraging, but still he hesitated. "I can't go back to the past, Ana. Things are different now."

She looked disappointed, but before they could say any more, one of the men called to him. "Hey, we need another pair of hands here."

"I've got to get back."

She reached out and touched his arm. "I'm not giving up, Vance. Can you give us one more chance? It's your choice what happens next."

He glanced away, not wanting her to see how she affected him. "I'll come by later. Meet me in the barn, say, four o'clock."

Ana smiled. "I'll be there." She walked off, leaving Vance aching to run after her.

Garrett came over. "So you worked things out?"

"We're just going to talk, later."

His friend sighed. "Take some advice. The less talking the better."

At four o'clock Ana walked out toward the barn and found Vance in the corral, with Rusty and Blondie saddled.

She nearly ran into his arms. "Hi."

He nodded. "Hi."

"Are we going somewhere?"

"I thought we'd go for a ride, somewhere we wouldn't draw so much attention."

Ana looked around and saw several of the men watching them. Good, she'd have him to herself. She took Blondie's reins from Vance and climbed on her mare.

Vance mounted Rusty, then together they walked the horses out the corral gate, thanking Todd for closing it.

It didn't take long before Ana picked up the pace and they were both racing across the pasture. She soon began to relax and enjoy her ride, not wanting to think that it could be their last one.

They rode past the alfalfa fields and Ana knew where Vance was directing her. It wasn't long before they ended up in the meadow, approaching the small cabin.

Once there, she pulled on Blondie's reins and the horse came to a stop. Vance did the same with Rusty. After tying the animals to the railing near the rebuilt lean-to, he went to the pump and began to fill the old trough with water.

Ana glanced around and noticed some subtle changes. The boards had been replaced on the porch floor, and there were new shingles on the roof, too.

Vance pulled a plastic cup from his saddlebag, filled it with water and offered it to her. "Here, this is so much better than bottled."

Ana drank about half, then gave it back, and he finished it. She wasn't feeling as sure about this talk as she'd been when they left twenty minutes ago. She looked out over the meadow, wishing it would give her some magic right now. Then suddenly the wind kicked up and clouds moved overhead, and soon came the raindrops.

"Come on. We better take cover." Vance grabbed her hand and pulled her onto the porch, then opened the door and got her inside the cabin.

"I guess we should have checked the weather," she said.

"It's not bad." Vance went to the small table and lit the kerosene lamp. "The rain should pass over in a few minutes."

Removing her hat, Ana wiped the moisture from her face and jeans jacket, then looked around. There were changes inside, too. The room had been cleaned for once. The bunks and old mattresses were gone, replaced by a large wrought-iron bed with a colorful quilt covering it. Her gaze quickly searched the rest of the room. The kitchen area had been cleaned, too. There were more canned goods on the shelves, and fresh curtains in the window.

"Who did this?"

He folded his arms across his chest and leaned against the sink counter. "It all depends, if you like it or not."

"What's not to like? Are you living here?"

He shook his head. "This is yours, Ana."

She felt her throat close up. "You did this for me? When?"

The rain continued to come down. "A few weeks ago," he told her. "I knew you liked to come here when you went riding, so I thought why not make it livable."

She walked to the bed. "Where did you find this?"

Vance wasn't sure he could pull this off. Being here with her was killing him. "It was in the barn, up in the attic." He paused. "It used to be mine, but the mattress is new. And I bought the quilt from Mrs. Hildebrand at the Country Days Festival."

"Oh, Vance." Ana's fingers traced the double wedding ring embroidered on the quilt. "How did you get everything out here?"

"In that old wagon behind the barn, and with a lot of help from Todd."

"But why?"

"I know what this place means to you, Ana." This was his chance. "And you mean a lot to me."

Her gaze rose to meet his, and Vance could see the glistening of tears.

"I don't deserve this," she choked out. "I said so many awful things to you."

He fought the urge to go over to her. They needed to talk first. "We both made mistakes. I should have told you about the land. Believe me, I tried. That night I came to your room, when you were going over the loan papers? I confessed it all to you, then realized you had fallen asleep before I finished my explanation. The next day was when Hoffman spilled the news to you at the bank."

Ana watched him. "I should have listened to you that day. I should have believed in you, I'm sorry for doubting you." She looked away. "I know I messed up everything. I drove you away from your home. Please believe that I never wanted to do that."

All at once the rain stopped and the sun came out. Ana released a long breath. "We should get back." She went toward the door.

Vance had to act quickly, and caught her before she got too far. He pushed the door closed easily. "You notice that I fixed the hinges? I even put a lock on the door." He slid the bolt to prove a point. "I'm not finished yet, Ana. I have a lot more to say to you."

She looked up at him, her eyes wide with hope, and with love. That gave him the courage to go on. "Eighteen years ago, I showed up at your house, that kid you and your sisters wanted nothing to do with."

When she started to speak, he raised his hand. "I need to say this, Ana." At her nod, he continued. "I didn't blame any of you for resenting me. So much of that was because of Colt, but we have to let that go, too. All I cared about for all those years was you. How much I wanted to see you every day."

"But after you kissed me that first time in the barn, you pushed me away."

"Colt would have thrown me so far off the ranch, I could never find my way back. I kept my distance, hoping that my feelings would fade away, like an adolescent infatuation." Vance shook his head. "They only got stronger, Ana. I couldn't stop caring about you even if I wanted to. And when you moved home this time, I knew I couldn't deny it any longer."

"Oh, Vance."

He shifted closer. "I care about you, Ana." He brushed his mouth cross hers. Once. Twice. "Do you want me to show you how much?"

She sucked in a breath. "Showing is good."

His mouth closed over hers, and he wrapped his arms around her waist and drew her against him. She whimpered and slid her hands up his chest, combing her fingers through his hair as she deepened the kiss. Finally he broke away.

His gaze met hers. "I love you, Analeigh Slater. I think I fell for you at fourteen, and never recovered."

"Oh, Vance, I love you so much." She rose up on her toes and kissed him again. "And I don't want you to ever recover from loving me. Because I never have. I know now that I loved you back then, too."

He cupped her face. "I don't plan to. And because of that love, I needed to give you back this land."

Ana hesitated, but knew they were both being honest, so she needed to say what she wanted. "No, we have to share it." She hesitated. "What were you planning to do with this meadow?"

He took her back to the window. "In a few years, I want to build a home here. Maybe start a small herd of Herefords, but my main love is horses, both breeding and training them."

"Funny, that's pretty much what I want to do, too."

He grinned at her, and a warm shiver raced through her. "I thought you had a career in town."

"I can multitask. I'm a Slater. There's ranching in my blood."

"I think there's a lot of stubbornness, too."

She loved the feel of Vance's arms around her. "And I don't plan on making anything easy for you, either. I wouldn't want you to get bored with me."

He grew serious. "That would never happen. I can't imagine my life without you in it, Ana." He smiled, but couldn't hide the nervousness. "I want to wake up every day with you. Live right here on this land where your ancestors settled a hundred years ago. I want children with your blue eyes and incredible beauty." He sank down on one knee on the old wooden floor. "Analeigh Maria Slater, will you marry me?"

Okay, that did it. She couldn't stop the tears as she nodded. "Oh, yes." She knelt down and wrapped her arms around Vance's neck. "Yes! Oh, yes, Vance, I'll marry you."

He kissed her, and by the time they broke apart, they were breathless. "Later, we'll go into Dillon and pick out a ring."

She could hardly wait to do that, then she remembered. "Oh, Colt comes home tomorrow. Maybe we should tell him first."

Vance smiled as they got to their feet. "Your father already knows how I feel about you." He grinned. "I think a better idea is staying here and enjoying the daylight we have left." He backed her up against the new double bed. "Don't you think we should celebrate our upcoming wedding?"

"As long as it's a private celebration."

His head lowered to hers. "Whatever the lady wants."

She took a teasing bite of his lip. "This lady wants you."

"I aim to please."

Ana wanted this time with her man in her special place. Now they'd both found somewhere they belonged.

Somewhere they could begin a life together, looking forward to another generation, in this magical place.

EPILOGUE

THE NEXT MORNING in the meadow, Vance and Ana walked out of the cabin. He drew his future bride into his arms and kissed her in the bright sunlight.

"I like how you say good-morning," she purred.

"And I liked how you said good-night." Vance recalled how he'd held Ana until dawn, and soon, they would be able to start their life together. "I'd keep you here longer, but I'm afraid they'll send out a search party."

He reluctantly released her, and they mounted the animals he'd saddled earlier, and headed toward the ranch. Once they arrived at the corral, several men looked in their direction.

Vance didn't care that everyone knew they'd spent the night together. Ana was going to be his wife, and if he had anything to say about it, they'd have a lot more stolen moments at the cabin. He had to agree with her, the meadow was magical.

"I think our secret's out," she said.

"You're not my secret, Ana. You're going to be my wife." He grinned. "And I want to shout it to the world."

Smiling, she climbed off her horse. "Well, my husband-to-be, I'd like to *shout* it to my family first. Do you mind?"

He came around Rusty. "Of course we should tell Colt and your sisters first." He stared into her blue eyes, and nearly lost it. He pulled her close. "You want me to tell them what a lucky guy I am? How much I love you?"

She reached up and touched his cheek. "No, just keep telling *me*." She brushed a kiss against his mouth. "Come on, let's go up to the house."

Once in the barn, they handed their horses over to Jake. The young man gave them a big smile and walked off with the mounts. In fact, they got several greetings along with smiles as they made their way to the house.

"I guess we never discussed what my job is," Vance said as they approached.

Ana stopped. "We want you to have your job back, of course. The Lazy S can't survive without you."

He loved the ranch, but he didn't just want to work for Slaters. "I think maybe I should invest in the operation."

She paused. "What do you mean?"

"If I'm going to be part of this family, I should contribute more. Make an investment in the future."

"You mean like money?"

He nodded. "I'm not some broken-down cowboy. I could invest in a few broodmares. I've managed to save some over the years."

She smiled, liking the idea. "That's nice to know. But you already own part of this ranch." When he started to dispute it, she raised a hand. "Why don't we discuss this with Colt?"

With that decided, they made their way up the drive to the back door and found Kathleen in the kitchen.

The older woman folded her arms over her chest. "I take it you couldn't get to a phone to tell me that you weren't coming home?"

Vance pulled Ana into a tight embrace. "I guess we were thinking about other things."

"It better be to tell me that you two have come to your senses."

Vance kissed Ana. "I think you can say that. How do you feel about helping with a wedding?"

Tears sprang to the housekeeper's eyes. "I've been waiting a long time for that to happen." She hugged Ana and then Vance. "Maybe that will get your sisters home."

Ana gasped. "Oh, no! Dad! We need to go get him." She checked her watch. "I have to shower first."

Kathleen held up her hands. "No need. Wade is escorting him home, along with Joel. You two just get cleaned up and give Colt the good news when he gets here. I think if anything will make him happy, this will." She rubbed her hands together. "Oh, it's going to be a good day. Now, you two run upstairs and get showered. I'll keep your breakfast warm."

"Yes, ma'am." Vance took Ana by the hand and they hurried through the house to the stairs, hearing Kathleen's words about no dallying. He stopped on the landing and kissed Ana. "I'm happy Colt is arriving home today, but I wanted to keep you all to myself for a while longer. You don't know how badly I want to steal you away and head back to the meadow."

Ana's gaze searched Vance's handsome face. She couldn't believe how much she loved this man. She also knew how close she'd come to losing him. "We'll go back to the cabin soon. Remember, we're going to build our home there."

"That has a lot to do with getting our business off the ground. How soon are you going to marry me?"

"Tomorrow?" she teased, but she was dead serious.

"Sounds great to me, but I think you'd be happier to have your sisters here for our wedding."

She arched an eyebrow. "Would you mind?"

He shook his head. "I'm just not sure your sisters are going to accept me into the family."

"That's their problem. You're the man I chose, the man I love. And if I know Tori, Josie and Marissa, they'll come around to love you, too."

Vance pulled Ana against him. "As far as I'm concerned, you're the only Slater sister that's important to me right now."

She smiled. "I'm the lucky sister." She brushed her mouth over his, stirring the flames. "Give it time. My sisters will grow on you."

He swung her up into his arms. "Like I said, you are the only one I want to marry, to be the mother of our children, to spend the rest of my life with."

"Oh, Vance. There's nothing I want more than to build a life with you."

He carried her down the hall to their room. There wasn't going to be "hers" or "his"; it was going to be "theirs" from now on.

Colt was pushed into the kitchen by Wade. He'd been home for a little over a day, and found he hated being in the wheelchair, but knew that he sometimes had to use it. But not for long, he decided. Now that he was finally home, he was going to recover. To get back as head of the ranch, head of his family. With some changes, of course.

Wade walked around him to the coffeemaker. "You need any help getting settled in?" his friend asked as he filled two mugs. He handed one to Colt.

"You d-don't have to hang around."

His friend arched an eyebrow. "Are you trying to get rid of me?"

Colt shook his head. "Get a life. You sp...ent too m-much time with me."

"I would like to think if this happened to me that you'd stick by me. We're friends, Colt. No matter how stubborn you are, or disagreeable, that will never change." The lawyer leaned back against the counter. "I only hope you take advantage of this second chance."

Colt smiled. He couldn't be happier. "Ana's marrying Vance."

Wade nodded. "I'd say that's a perfect match. But you still have to repair the problems with your three other daughters. You got any ideas?"

He held up a finger. "One at a time. I learned my lesson."

"It's about time."

Two days later, Vance walked out of the barn and saw Ana's car pulling up at the house. He picked up his pace and got to her as she was climbing out of the driver's side. He leaned down and kissed her.

"Oh, I like this kind of welcome home," she told him as she let him have her briefcase.

"Always. How was your first day back at school?"

She kissed him again. "Well, outside of talking about you, and showing off my new engagement ring—" she flashed the square-cut diamond on her left hand "—there wasn't time for much else." She grinned. "Have I told you how much I love the ring and what a special guy you are?"

He nodded. There was a time when Vance hadn't felt special. Hadn't felt he belonged. It was Ana who made him feel as if he could do anything. "I always want to be that guy for you, Ana."

She pressed her lips to his. "Just love me, Vance. No one else does that as well as you do. And I couldn't love another man as much as I love you."

He placed his head against hers. "I love you, Ana. We're going to make such a great life together."

The look in her eyes told him she believed in him. That was all he needed, that and her love.

He kissed her again—a kiss so sweet he didn't even hear another car pull up. When they finally broke apart, he noticed a familiar-looking woman climb out.

She was small, with sandy-brown hair, and they were close enough that he could see those Slater-blue eyes.

Ana gasped. "Oh, my God, Josie."

Her younger sister came around the car, staring at them both. "I guess I surprised you."

"What are you doing home?" Ana asked.

"I thought you said you needed help with Colt." She continued to watch Vance. "And there seem to be some things you left out." A tiny smile tugged at the corners of her younger sister's mouth. "How many other surprises are there that I don't know about?"

Ana shot a glance at Vance and caught his wink as he drew her close to his side. "Let's just start out with saying welcome home, Josie. And secondly, it seems Ana and I are going to need your services as an event planner." He gave her a big smile. "Do you do weddings?"

* * * * *

Mills & Boon® Hardback
August 2013

ROMANCE

The Billionaire's Trophy	Lynne Graham
Prince of Secrets	Lucy Monroe
A Royal Without Rules	Caitlin Crews
A Deal with Di Capua	Cathy Williams
Imprisoned by a Vow	Annie West
Duty At What Cost?	Michelle Conder
The Rings that Bind	Michelle Smart
An Inheritance of Shame	Kate Hewitt
Faking It to Making It	Ally Blake
Girl Least Likely to Marry	Amy Andrews
The Cowboy She Couldn't Forget	Patricia Thayer
A Marriage Made in Italy	Rebecca Winters
Miracle in Bellaroo Creek	Barbara Hannay
The Courage To Say Yes	Barbara Wallace
All Bets Are On	Charlotte Phillips
Last-Minute Bridesmaid	Nina Harrington
Daring to Date Dr Celebrity	Emily Forbes
Resisting the New Doc In Town	Lucy Clark

MEDICAL

Miracle on Kaimotu Island	Marion Lennox
Always the Hero	Alison Roberts
The Maverick Doctor and Miss Prim	Scarlet Wilson
About That Night...	Scarlet Wilson

Mills & Boon® Large Print

August 2013

ROMANCE

Master of her Virtue	Miranda Lee
The Cost of her Innocence	Jacqueline Baird
A Taste of the Forbidden	Carole Mortimer
Count Valieri's Prisoner	Sara Craven
The Merciless Travis Wilde	Sandra Marton
A Game with One Winner	Lynn Raye Harris
Heir to a Desert Legacy	Maisey Yates
Sparks Fly with the Billionaire	Marion Lennox
A Daddy for Her Sons	Raye Morgan
Along Came Twins...	Rebecca Winters
An Accidental Family	Ami Weaver

HISTORICAL

The Dissolute Duke	Sophia James
His Unusual Governess	Anne Herries
An Ideal Husband?	Michelle Styles
At the Highlander's Mercy	Terri Brisbin
The Rake to Redeem Her	Julia Justiss

MEDICAL

The Brooding Doc's Redemption	Kate Hardy
An Inescapable Temptation	Scarlet Wilson
Revealing The Real Dr Robinson	Dianne Drake
The Rebel and Miss Jones	Annie Claydon
The Son that Changed his Life	Jennifer Taylor
Swallowbrook's Wedding of the Year	Abigail Gordon

Mills & Boon® Hardback
September 2013

ROMANCE

Challenging Dante	Lynne Graham
Captivated by Her Innocence	Kim Lawrence
Lost to the Desert Warrior	Sarah Morgan
His Unexpected Legacy	Chantelle Shaw
Never Say No to a Caffarelli	Melanie Milburne
His Ring Is Not Enough	Maisey Yates
A Reputation to Uphold	Victoria Parker
A Whisper of Disgrace	Sharon Kendrick
If You Can't Stand the Heat...	Joss Wood
Maid of Dishonour	Heidi Rice
Bound by a Baby	Kate Hardy
In the Line of Duty	Ami Weaver
Patchwork Family in the Outback	Soraya Lane
Stranded with the Tycoon	Sophie Pembroke
The Rebound Guy	Fiona Harper
Greek for Beginners	Jackie Braun
A Child to Heal Their Hearts	Dianne Drake
Sheltered by Her Top-Notch Boss	Joanna Neil

MEDICAL

The Wife He Never Forgot	Anne Fraser
The Lone Wolf's Craving	Tina Beckett
Re-awakening His Shy Nurse	Annie Claydon
Safe in His Hands	Amy Ruttan

0813 GEN STD HB

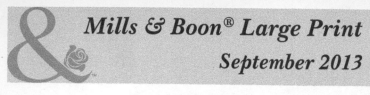

Mills & Boon® Large Print
September 2013

ROMANCE

A Rich Man's Whim	Lynne Graham
A Price Worth Paying?	Trish Morey
A Touch of Notoriety	Carole Mortimer
The Secret Casella Baby	Cathy Williams
Maid for Montero	Kim Lawrence
Captive in his Castle	Chantelle Shaw
Heir to a Dark Inheritance	Maisey Yates
Anything but Vanilla...	Liz Fielding
A Father for Her Triplets	Susan Meier
Second Chance with the Rebel	Cara Colter
First Comes Baby...	Michelle Douglas

HISTORICAL

The Greatest of Sins	Christine Merrill
Tarnished Amongst the Ton	Louise Allen
The Beauty Within	Marguerite Kaye
The Devil Claims a Wife	Helen Dickson
The Scarred Earl	Elizabeth Beacon

MEDICAL

NYC Angels: Redeeming The Playboy	Carol Marinelli
NYC Angels: Heiress's Baby Scandal	Janice Lynn
St Piran's: The Wedding!	Alison Roberts
Sydney Harbour Hospital: Evie's Bombshell	Amy Andrews
The Prince Who Charmed Her	Fiona McArthur
His Hidden American Beauty	Connie Cox